The Other Side of Silence

Stories by George Harrar

"If we had a keen vision and feeling of all ordinary human life, it would be like hearing the grass grow and the squirrel's heart beat, and we should die of that roar which lies on the other side of silence."

— George Eliot, *Middlemarch*

Stephen Durkee Books 2025

DEDICATION

To Linda, my wife and personal editor

Softcover ISBN 979-8-9888717-3-6

Epub   ISBN 979-8-9888717-4-3

Stephen Durkee Books 2025

ACKNOWLEDGEMENTS

Gentle Breezes—*Story Quarterly*

The 5:22—Carson McCullers prizewinner,
Story magazine, & *Best American Short Stories, 1999*

The River Ocean—*Reed Magazine*

In Memoriam--*American Way Magazine*

The Lake Region Poetry Club—*Sideshow Anthology*

The Dreaming Man—*Eclectic Literary Forum*

The Surprise Hit of an Otherwise Lackluster Season—
DASH Journal

Bedlam--*Gemini* prizewinner

Cover photo courtesy of longtime friend and col-
league, Glenn Rifkin

The author gratefully acknowledges the assistance
at every stage of the publication process of Stephen
Durkee, publisher and former roommate at New York
University

Praise for Fiction by George Harrar

The Spinning Man
"(An) elegant and unnerving mystery of psychological suspense...(Harrar is) a graceful and subtle writer."
— *New York Times Book Review*

"A taut psychological drama...blends the commonplace and the esoteric with exceptional ease."
— *Boston Globe*

"Suspenseful...plot and an unblinking look at the tensions of family life..."-- *Washington Post*

Reunion at Red Paint Bay
"Harrar skillfully echoes Alfred Hitchcock's theme about how a seemingly innocent man can be sucked into a disturbing vortex of forces that lie just below the surface of 'normal' life." —*Kirkus Reviews*

"Harrar is one of those writers on the verge of connecting with a much larger audience; this could be his moment." –*Booklist*

Parents Wanted
"A killer read."—*Kirkus Reviews*

INTRODUCTION

The Other Side of Silence is a collection of short fiction by award-winning writer George Harrar.

The stories include "The 5:22," which won the Carson McCullers Prize from *Story* magazine and was selected for the 1999 edition of *Best American Short Stories.* Also included are stories that appeared in *Story Quarterly, Sideshow Anthology, Reed Magazine, DASH, Eclectic Literary Forum,* and *Gemini Magazine* (prize-winner).

"Chapter One" is the beginning of *Blue Hour*, a story of resilience by a boy in a wildly dysfunctional family. The novel is available for publication.

A half-dozen new, unpublished stories complete the collection.

"The 5:22" received dramatic readings at the American Repertory Theater in Cambridge, Symphony Space in New York City and the Williamstown Theatre in Williamstown, Mass. It was also featured in the LiveWriters podcast read by actor LeVar Burton.

Part One

Stories in which....

A funeral director realizes he may be too good at preparing bodies for viewing;

An engineer's well-planned life seems to fall apart;

A long-time resident of a retirement home finds her voice—and it's a scream;

A hardware salesman takes up an unlikely pursuit—writing poetry;

A dream veers perilously close to reality;

Two stalwarts of the community, a most incompatible couple, die and leave townspeople at odds over how to interpret their generous bequest; and

An old man manages to meet expectations.

The River Ocean

Rose Stanton looks good enough to sip English Breakfast on her patio, play a few hands of rummy, perhaps even stroll out to her garden to smell the lilacs just in bloom. Tap her on the shoulder and she'd wake up, raring to go. Anyone who didn't know her would guess she was no older than 85, maybe even 80, and that makes Dylan McElroy proud. He's employed everything in his work kit to get her this way--the plastic eye caps, the mouth tacks, the new lip glue. He packed her sagging breasts with tissue paper to give them a modestly rounded shape. He layered on skin builder to thicken her neck. Instead of calling in his usual makeup woman, he spent an hour doing the facial cosmetics himself. With the shell pink gloss on her lips, the faintest rouge to her cheeks and the capped front teeth, Rose looks better dead than alive. What more could anyone ask?

* * * * *

As far as restorations go, this one challenged even

Dylan's considerable talents. If only people appreciated how hard it is to renovate a body that has lived
on this rough earth for 100 years. And for viewing in a
short sleeve dress--what did the family think, that the
bruises from her IVs would magically disappear post
mortem?

Dylan moisturizes the long skeletal fingers with
Vaseline Intensive Care to soften them should one
of her children reach into the casket for a tender
squeeze. Then he places the hands right on top of left,
palm over knuckles, as is his habit. But studying them
like that for a moment, the position doesn't seem
natural on Rose, so he crosses them the other way, left
over right.

He scoops out a fingerful of restorative wax from
the tub sitting on his work tray and lets it warm in
his hand for a moment. On the near wall hangs the
picture of Rose he had to work from, her head slightly
bowed as if embarrassed at being photographed and
perhaps a little annoyed at all the fuss. He imagines
her thinking, *There, I've done it, I'm 100. Now pull
the plug and let me go!* He likes that the Stanton family submitted this last image of her to the newspaper.
So many obituary pictures make the deceased look
preternaturally young and lively, as if they dropped
dead mid-stride on the way to some pleasant engage-
ment. That's not the way it usually is at all. Most people see death coming. A few, like Rose, even welcome

it in the door. And she met her fate in better shape than most much younger, her backbone straight, her hair full and wavy, her skin amazingly tight on her face, just a pinch of elasticity. She couldn't avoid the wrinkles, though. Her face reminds him of a finely cracked mirror, but not one so broken that you would throw it away.

Dylan dabs the wax on Rose's neck and it hardens against the cold flesh, covering over the slice of his scalpel. He reopens his kit and pulls out a syringe. He dips it into the vial of tissue builder and extracts a few drops. With his left hand steadying his right, he pokes the needle into the corners of Rose's eyes and squirts behind the eyeballs. He does the same inside both nostrils and below her lip. Immediately the skin fills up, and the wrinkles flatten out a bit. Rose is almost glowing now. The effect wouldn't last long, but he was just curious to see how the tissue builder would work on the oldest body he had ever encountered. He could be confident now injecting her again just prior to the viewing.

She looks elegant in her lavender gown, the one her son said she wore to her fiftieth anniversary party a quarter century ago. It was no small feat for Dylan to squeeze her into the satin dress without snipping open the back. Some funeral directors would take their scissors to the material without the slightest thought. But the idea that a person would lie forever in clothes slit along their spine unsettled him, like dressing them without their underwear. He just couldn't do it.

As he repacks his supplies, Dylan anticipates the comments at the viewing. More than a few people would say that Rose never looked so good. Some would laugh nervously at how lifelike she seemed-- none of that waxy pallor or frozen expression. Everyone would agree that she was going out of this world in first-class shape, and that is Dylan's reward.

Prompt payment is appreciated, too, of course. A kind word from the eldest child is always nice, and perhaps a well-chosen card a few days later from one or another of the daughters. He would like very much to have them write that he worked a miracle.

* * * * *

Rose's son arrived unannounced the following day. Dylan was up to his wrists in embalming fluid at the time, hooking his trusty PortiBoy pump to an obese gentleman of fifty-two. Frank Stanton would have to wait.

Mercifully, the family had chosen to keep the casket closed on this oversized father of four. Still, his wife, a surprisingly petite woman, had insisted on the embalming as something he would have wanted. Dylan thought that an odd way to phrase it, but $450 for two hours' work was good money even if he did need to use an extra gallon of gluteraldehyde. He watched the pink liquid pump through the arteries, pushing the blood ahead of it out of the tube stuck in the man's jugular vein. There was the familiar gurgling in the sink, the sound Dylan always heard in his head when people complained that their life "was going down the drain." If they only knew.

As usual during basic plumbing jobs like this one, his mind began to wander. He thought of Lazarus, his favorite Biblical character. How did he look after waking from the dead? And what happened when he died the second time--did his friends give him a proper burial all over again, or did they expect him to rise that time, too? Dylan thought of the Greeks' flat, round earth, surrounded by the swirling River Ocean. On the far shore of this great encircling water, just beyond the setting sun, there was Hades, the realm of the dead. *On this side the living, over there, the departed.* That was simple enough. How had life and death become so complicated? People searching for something to say to him at social gatherings often asked, "What do *you* think happens after death?" as if working on the dead gave him special insight as to where they were headed next. He never offered an opinion except to say that every earthly form should be well outfitted for the trip, wherever it led.

At least once during each embalming session, he forced himself to imagine the body lying stiff on the porcelain table as a loved one. With someone you cared about there could be no rough handling to distribute the fluid through the limbs. A gentle massage was called for. You wouldn't turn on the radio to some mindless talk station as you jabbed a trocar into the stomach cavity and turned on the suction. You wouldn't allow an assistant to come in inquiring about an inconsequential matter as you sprayed the body with germicide. Dylan prided himself on treating the deceased as a member of the family, and he knew well what it was like to handle relatives. During his 21 years in the business he had worked on both grandfathers, three aunts and assorted cousins. What he could never envision was embalming his wife, Christine. That would be too much for him to expect of himself. But was it better to leave such intimate work to others? Where was the love in that, to have some other embalmer cut into her, drain her, stuff her and zip her back up again?

Dylan finished flushing and filling Gregory Gorski, the 300-pounder on the table. It was a lucky break that the giant man had suffered his massive coronary so early in the morning, right after his shower and shave. That saved some cleanup work. With little in the way of aesthetics to be done, it was a convenient time to break. He peeled off his latex gloves and went out to greet Frank Stanton.

Dylan was surprised to see an elderly gentleman seated in the reception room. The tall, thin fellow rose to his feet with some effort and offered his hand, which was mottled with age spots. Of course this made sense--the children of Rose Stanton were not children at all.

Mr. Stanton held out rosary beads and a book of photos. "I brought these for Mother," he said. "I think she'd like to take them with her."

Dylan acknowledged this thoughtful gesture with a slight nod. "I'm sure they'll be a comfort to her." It was a handy phrase, suitable for all sorts of occasions when the deceased's relatives showed up with such things. But he never knew what to do next. Should he look at the pictures, ask who is who, admire the family? Or were these private memories of a life that required no comment from him? Dylan waited for some signal as to whether Rose's son considered an undertaker a friend of the family or just a man providing an essential service, ferryman to the underworld.

Mr. Stanton nodded at the photos. "I know it's foolish, but they meant something to her."

"It's not foolish at all," Dylan said, which was another phrase he used quite often, even when the request was downright foolish. Like the woman who wanted her husband laid out in his Speedo, or the man who insisted on having a portable radio, with long-life batteries, placed in the casket by his ear, tuned to the station carrying the ball games. Dylan interpreted Mr. Stanton's comment about the pictures as permission, perhaps even encouragement, to peruse them. "They're very nice," he said as he leafed through the dozen small, faded prints. He saw Rose grow from a little girl riding in a carriage through the snow to an old woman in a wheelchair with a paper crown on her head saying "100." It startled him a bit to see a life go by so quickly.

"It was a struggle," Mr. Stanton said, "but she made it to the century mark--that was her goal."

It didn't surprise Dylan that Rose had reached such a milestone, then succumbed the following week. "Women often die right after their birthdays," he said, "men right before. I see it all the time."

"Is that so?" Mr. Stanton said, but Dylan could tell he wasn't much interested in this trivial fact of human nature. "You'll make sure then," the son said, "to put the pictures into her casket, I mean?"

"Certainly," Dylan said, "or you could do it yourself right now, if you'd like.

"That's possible?"

Dylan smiled at the implication that he could make the seemingly impossible so easily possible. He led the elderly son through the No Admittance door into the back room, and Mr. Stanton's hard shoes squeaked strangely on the wood floor. When they came to the casket, Dylan let his hand fall for a moment on the beautiful roses etched into the cherry. He often found some reason to stall here. A private viewing like this was not to be rushed. Then with slow, precise movements, he opened the lid.

The sight took the man's breath away. He reached out with one hand to steady himself on the side of the casket. "It's how I remember her from years ago, before...before she got so old."

"She's an attractive woman," Dylan said, using the present tense, as he always did when referring to the newly departed.

With shaky hands Mr. Stanton lay the pictures on his mother's rounded chest and slipped the string of rosary beads between her fingers. "She feels so cold. Mother always hated the cold."

"The fire has gone out inside her," Dylan explained as gently as he could. What he meant was, she's at room temperature.

Mr. Stanton exhaled deeply. "Well, I guess she's ready to rest now. I'm glad I had this last chance to see her."

Dylan started to close the lid, but Frank's words resounded in his head—*I'm glad I had this last chance to see her.* "Of course," he reminded, "you'll have the opportunity again at the wake tomorrow."

Mr. Stanton looked confused. "My sister, she didn't reach you?"

"No."

"Well, I'm sorry, but you see, it's just that the family talked it over last night, and we decided against the viewing."

Dylan held the lid halfway closed, not quite believing what he had just heard. Was his handiwork to be viewed by only one person, this old man with the decaying hands? That wasn't right. Not after he had paid such attention to her hair, to her eyes, to her cheeks. *Look at her*, he wanted to say, *look at how I transformed this withered old lady into the mother you remembered. Why wouldn't you want the world to see her now?*

"You did request an open casket," he said as he eased the heavy lid down on Rose Stanton. "As you can see, I took great care to prepare her for that."

Mr. Stanton touched Dylan's arm, and Dylan recognized the gesture as one of dismissive reassurance. "I appreciate your work. She looks amazing. It's just that my sisters and I discussed the matter, and we don't think it's not tasteful nowadays to...."

Dylan couldn't listen to any more. He despised the insinuation that there was anything distasteful about restoring a person for her final public appearance. He had heard that opinion once too often lately. He supposed he shouldn't care. It wasn't his loved one, after all. If they wanted cremation, give them cremation. If they wanted him to lay the naked corpse outside on a holy tower for the vultures to devour in some unnerving Parsi ritual, then he would oblige that wish as well, government regulations permitting, of course.

"...So you see," Mr. Stanton continued, "that's why we decided against having an open casket."

"Perhaps you could have decided this a bit earlier," Dylan said. His tone was sharper than he normally used with a grieving family, but he couldn't quite temper his displeasure at this turn of events.

Mr. Stanton nodded vaguely. "I guess we were just going along with what you said was traditional. But we got to talking last night, going over the last details, you know, and it came out that none of us really wanted people to see her like that."

Dylan considered pressing his argument, perhaps recounting great wakes of the past where the dearly departed seemed to come alive again, as if lying on a lavish throne, the guest of honor at one last party. You couldn't get that feeling with a closed casket, could you? Even with a somber Protestant viewing in the narthex before the service, why, he could pull out dozens of thank-you cards from people saying that having the casket open was the smartest thing they had ever done. A viewing affirmed that a person had indeed died, not just disappeared one day like an old sock. A viewing allowed the grief of one to be shared by all. Didn't Kubler-Ross say that? Who knew more about dying than she?

Dylan assessed all of the arguments he could make and said nothing. He could sense lost causes and this was one of them. Perhaps he could convince this one son, but there wasn't time to change the mind of a whole family.

Mr. Stanton took off his glasses and wiped his cloudy eyes. He said again that their decision had nothing to do with Dylan's work, which was topnotch. And of course, they expected to pay for his services just as if the casket were open.

Dylan tried to smile, but he felt like scowling, and that made him wonder, which expression was winning on his face? All that work for nothing. Was there any other art like this where someone could put in so much of himself and his workmanship not see the light of day? He didn't think so.

It wasn't the first time this had happened. He figured that of his 1,400-odd embalmings, perhaps 20 times relatives had changed their minds about the viewing at the last hour. So what bothered him so much this time? Was he just being prideful about making a centenarian look so good? Or was the increasing squeamishness of people to look death in the face finally getting to him? He had to ask himself, whom was he working for, the living or the dead?

Dylan escorted Mr. Stanton to the office, took his check for $7,725--payment in full--and then led him to the front door. The bright sun of the afternoon flooded the hallway for a moment, and Dylan blinked in the sudden light. Mr. Stanton repeated how happy he was with the work, and how happy his brothers

and sister would be if they had seen it, and how happy
his mother would be--how happy she *is*, he corrected
himself.

For the first time in his embalming life, Dylan was
sick of hearing the compliments. The phone rang in
the office, and he made some gesture to indicate that
he had to go.

* * * * *

"Mr. McElroy," the caller said, "this is Sgt. Burns at
the station. We've got a bad one for you."

Dylan shuddered at the words, yet they excited
him, too. The "bad ones" were almost always car
accidents--drinkers and speeders wrapping themselves around trees or telephone poles. His stomach
tightened at first sight of the victims with their slashed
faces, broken necks and mangled limbs. But he was
proud that the police called him for the cases other
undertakers in town preferred not to handle.

He hopped into his van and hurried to Women's
Hospital. He drove around the back, weaving past
the Dumpsters and broken-down ambulances and
mounds of construction dirt. He backed into the space
by the unmarked black door and then walked around
to the main entrance. As he strode down the long hall-
ways, he waved discreetly to the various orderlies he
passed, careful not to arouse too much interest among
the patients. He would not want anyone to inquire
what this man's business was in the hospital.

Dylan signed in at Pathology, and the receptionist gave him a key tied to a crinkled piece of cardboard marked "Morgue." "No need for the guard to go with you, Mr. McElroy," she said, "there's only one in the cooler right now."

He passed the elevator and took the stairs one flight down. He unlocked the outer door of the morgue and pulled on his gloves. Then he opened the refrigerated vault, took a deep breath, and entered. He checked the thermometer on the wall--42degrees, at least four degrees too warm. He would have to talk to the hospital about proper preservation. Luckily, he was getting his body out quickly.

On the nearest stretcher, a human form swelled under a white cotton shroud. Dylan pushed the sheet up from the feet and reached for the toe tag. The black block letters said, "Jennifer R. Straitch." Such a young woman, with all of her life ahead of her. It saddened him to know she hadn't seen death coming, that she had no chance to step out of the way. Surprise, he often thought, was the aspect of mortality that he objected to most.

* * * * *

Dylan waited till next morning before contacting the Straitch family. There was no rush to decide things, he told the mother several times over the phone, but she insisted on coming down immediately.

As he waited for her, Dylan picked up the Discover

magazine with the article he had been meaning to read: "Funeral Directors--A Dying Profession." He didn't appreciate the double entendre in the headline. But as he read he realized that there was more meaning to it than just the pun. Scientists were predicting that within 50 years they could implant multiple artificial parts into aging humans, turning them into a mixture of plastic and metal and flesh that might live for ages.

The prospect of this didn't please him. He didn't care about his business--he was sure to be long gone himself before medicine prevailed over death, and he had no heir. He feared for human existence itself. What kind of story would life be without the promise of a timely ending? Would anyone really choose everlasting existence?

* * * * *

When he opened the front door of his funeral home a half hour later, he was shocked. The woman standing before him in the dark grey dress looked so much like the body lying twisted and torn on his table inside.

"I'm Carolyn Straitch," she said. "You have my daughter."

It was a strange way to put it, but she was right--of all the people on earth, he had her 18-year-old daughter. What were the odds of that 24 hours ago? The woman's face was puffy from crying and her eyes drooped with tiredness, but she still seemed lovely to him. He had seen others like this, always women, on whom sadness was beautiful. On men, sadness was just sad.

She turned sideways and tipped her head to the small car parked at an odd angle in the semi-circle of the driveway. In the passenger's side, a man slumped against the door. "Do you need my husband for this?" she asked.

"Not at all," Dylan said.

Mrs. Straitch took his hand and thanked him for responding so quickly to the call from the police. They were new in town, she said, and had no idea where to turn.

It's my job to respond quickly, he thought, but of course he wouldn't say this. A mother would not want to hear that her daughter had become merely a job for anyone, let alone a stranger. He said, "I'm ready to help any way I can."

Dylan led her into his sitting room and talked her through his list of services, from body preparation, dressing and casketing, to placing the obituary, opening the grave and interment. For the box, he offered her cherry and mahogany as well as metal ones, sealed and unsealed. He described the choice of bedding and liners, such as satin or velvet.

She glanced at her little yellow pad, where she had been taking notes. "Sealed metal," she said, "what would be the advantage of that?"

"A sealed metal casket protects the body from air," he said simply.

"Forever?"

Nothing lasts forever, Dylan thought, so why would someone expect a casket to? "Not forever," he said, "but it does come with a guarantee of replacement, if it ever proves defective."

Mrs. Straitch laughed oddly, he thought, and leaned across his desk. "Under what circumstances, Mr. McElroy, might we learn that the casket had become defective?"

Dylan felt defensive. He didn't like the implication that he was offering unnecessary options. "Limited circumstances, to be sure," he said. "But for instance, if the body ever needs to be moved from one cemetery to another."

"We won't worry about that now," she said as she put her pen and pad back in her pocketbook. "An unsealed metal casket will be fine, but it must be ready for the funeral the day after tomorrow. My husband is not bearing up well, so I want to get everything over with quickly."

Dylan nodded that he understood. She stood up and he did, too. "There is one more matter," he said. "What are your thoughts about a viewing?"

She looked at him curiously. "Is that advisable--I mean, in her condition?"

Dylan liked to think that he hadn't met a body he

couldn't make presentable for a viewing, but that was exaggeration. He couldn't restore a face where the skin had been burned away. He could rebuild a bit of an ear or nose out of wax, but not the whole thing. There were limits to what he could do in a few days. In this case, though, he had an attractive young girl to work with. The worst of the accident could be covered by a dress, and he was sure he could make the lacerations disappear from her cheeks with surface restorer. People might even ask themselves, *Why did she have to die? She doesn't appear injured at all.*

"Yes," Dylan said confidently, "she will look fine for a viewing."

Mrs. Straitch blinked rapidly, and he wondered if this was some new habit, perhaps a small glimpse of a restless soul twitching beneath her calm exterior. "Then that is what we want," she said.

"Are you sure? I mean, with your husband so upset, I don't want to talk you into anything."

"She was a beautiful girl, Mr. McElroy. We want everyone to see that."

Dylan took her arm. "Your daughter will be beautiful forever."

* * * * *

In the chapel of the old Methodist church, Dylan leaned against the wall by the side door and watched the relatives and friends of Jennifer Straitch pass by her casket. Several spoke to her, which was a good sign. A few slipped small items over the rim of the box. One young man--the boyfriend?--broke into sobs, and the tears flicked off his face. Later he'll be glad he saw her like this, Dylan assured himself.

From the sanctuary of the church, organ music began, and he checked his watch. It was just a few minutes before 7 o'clock, starting time for the service. Everything was running smoothly. At the end of the viewing line, Carolyn Straitch and her husband approached the casket. Dylan was surprised to see a solidly built gentleman in his mid-50s, with broad shoulders and thick hands. He had assumed a smaller man, one who was too frail to even enter the funeral home.

Mrs. Straitch led her husband by the arm to the casket. Dylan leaned to his left to see their faces at the exact moment they laid eyes on their daughter. He saw the mother's hand grip the side of the casket. He saw her head tilt a little, as one might look at an adorable baby in a crib. He saw her smile.

A smile! Dylan couldn't have hoped for more.

Now it was the father's turn to step up, and what Dylan saw was the most bizarre expression he had ever witnessed on a human face. What was it--confusion, bewilderment? Yes, but more than that. It was the look of a man struggling mightily to make sense of what lay before his eyes. Dylan thought of the Apostle Paul peering across the mysterious swirling waters into the world of the dead. It would take a moment to understand.

Mr. Straitch looked away from the casket and mumbled something. Dylan stepped forward, ready to be of service. Perhaps one of the visitors had placed something inappropriate in the box.

"I knew she wasn't gone," Mr. Straitch said to his wife. "Why did you say she was gone?"

Carolyn took his hand in hers and tried to move him away. "Jenny is gone, John, believe me."

He pulled out of her grasp and gazed at his daughter again. "No, she's sleeping," he said, "just sleeping."

Dylan had heard this observation before and always took it as a compliment. Certainly she was sleeping, an endless sweet repose, the sleep that does not wake.

Mr. Straitch reached over the edge of the casket. Dylan had seen this happen many times as well, fathers clutching the hands of their daughters, mothers running their fingers over the cold cheeks of their sons--some last touch that would make up for all the embraces lost in the hurriedness of time. He closed his eyes and imagined for a moment standing over his own dead wife. What would his final gesture be? What final touch?

The music from the sanctuary grew louder. Dylan opened his eyes--Mr. Straitch was draped over the side of the casket now. Dylan thought he might have collapsed, but in a moment he rose up, holding his daughter in his arms.

"I'll take her home now," he said.

"John, no, put her down," Mrs. Straitch said gently, but her words had no power over him.

"She shouldn't wake up here," he said as he shifted the body in his arms. Long brown hair fell back over the crook of his arm. Legs stuck out stiffly. He glanced around the chapel, saw the side door near Dylan, and started toward it. The few relatives remaining in the room parted for him. "She's sleeping," he assured them as he passed by. "Just sleeping."

Mr. Straitch approached, his face almost cheerful, without any strain of holding the dead weight of his only child. He saw Dylan and nodded toward the closed door. "Would you be so kind?"

For the first time in his professional life, Dylan didn't know what to do. It was his job to be kind, of course, but what would kindness be in this situation?

Mr. Straitch shifted the heaviness in his hands and awkwardly reached for the knob himself. Dylan foresaw the horrible possibilities. What if he dropped her? What if someone tried to stop him and he became violent? Dylan was not a father himself, had never been blessed with his own sweet child, but he could imagine holding onto her like this, cradling her close to his chest like a helpless infant. How could he ever let go?

"Allow me," he said as he opened the door, and

Mr. Straitch swept his cold, stiff daughter out into the warm evening air.

The 5:22

For more than a year Walter Mason and the woman with one ear nodded to each other at 5:22 p.m., or thereabouts, when the Western Local pulled into Lincoln Station. As he descended the steep metal steps clutching his briefcase, she would be standing near last in the small line of passengers waiting on the wooden platform to board. If it were lightly raining or snowing, she might hold a newspaper over her head. Sometimes she turned her face to the sky and opened her mouth a little, as if thirsty. In heavy rain she held a small yellow umbrella while the others waited under the eaves of nearby shops. She always carried an overstuffed white shopping bag, but nothing ever protruded from the top to hint at what was inside.

Her complexion was dark, perhaps Mediterranean or Middle Eastern. But she dressed as any American woman might, in a blouse and skirt, or pants and sweater. Invariably, though, she wore a colorful scarf around her head, wrapped delicately, it seemed to Walter, as one would a bouquet or some other live thing.

The scarf covered, of course, the missing right

ear, as Walter assumed it was meant to do. He would never have known of the deformity if a gust of wind one afternoon had not whipped the scarf suddenly free of her head. She dropped her purse and shopping bag and fumbled to secure the fine silk under her chin. Then she looked up and saw his rude stare. It was awful of him, he knew that, and he averted his eyes. What had possessed him to gaze at her for those few seconds that the crimson scarf fluttered in the wind, revealing the thick, slashing scars of an ear that wasn't there anymore?

* * * * *

When the woman didn't appear on the platform the following Monday, Walter didn't think much of it. She had missed other days over the last year--he could recall two for sure. But both were during snowstorms, it occurred to him as he crossed the rutted dirt parking lot, not on unusually warm spring days such as this. He opened the door of his Saab to let the day's hot air exhale from the car. Then it came to him-- perhaps she had not appeared today because he had noticed her missing ear the Friday before.

It charmed Walter to think of this woman as being so shy. He was shy himself. He hadn't married even though he was 47 and interested--that in itself would demonstrate a lagging sense of forwardness. He did cheerfully submit to the blind dates arranged for him through the unstinting efforts of the married women

at the Institute. But they remained one-time affairs-
-or rather more precisely, one-time intersections of
two people looking for something other than what
they found.

What was he looking for? A certain sweetness of
temperament was uppermost on his list, a flexible
mind (though not one incapable of holding a firm
opinion), and perhaps a sense of mankind's insig-
nificance in the totality of the universe. The ability
to apply order to the world would also be handy in a
wife. These attributes, which he obligingly scrawled
down as an aid to the matchmakers in his department, were apparently no help at all. They wanted to
know what he desired in height and weight, profession, previous marital status and post-marital attach-
ments, such as children. He supposed it was curious
that he never thought in those terms, but there it
was. He didn't care about shape, occupation or legal
connections, just as he hoped a woman wouldn't care
that he was unfit in the athletic sense of the word,
underemployed for the number of degrees appended
to his name, and suspiciously unattached for all of his
adult years. He didn't try to camouflage the gray in his
hair or wear the kind of tailored suits that would slim
down the excesses of his appetite. Though he was not
overly proud of his condition, he was at least comfortable with it. But if he had only one ear, he wondered,
what would he do, without a scarf to hide the terrible

secret?

* * * * *

The woman didn't appear on Tuesday as well, Walter concluded with some certainty that she had begun a week's vacation. Each succeeding day that the train arrived at 5:22 and she was not there only stiffened his reasoning. On Thursday, cold rain draped the region, and Walter found himself lamenting that the woman's time off might be spoiled by inclement weather. Perhaps, though, she was a reader and would be happy enough within doors. When he leafed through the New York Times Book Review that Sunday, he imagined her vacation reading list, possibly a book on exotic foods, such as "Bengali Cooking," or an intimate collection of short stories, such as "Women in Their Beds." For a lingering moment, Walter pictured her as the woman on the cover of that book, with her long black hair languishing on the pillow and one breast peeking above the sheet.

* * * * *

It was with some anticipation on the following Monday that Walter rose from his usual seat and hurried along the aisle even before the train began its slow braking into Lincoln. He reached the heavy sliding door just as Mel, the conductor, opened it from the other side and called out, "Next Stop, Lincoln. That's Lincoln, Next Stop."

Walter squeezed past him so he would have a

good view out of the open car. "Where's the fire?" Mel asked.

"Oh, no fire, Mel," Walter answered with a little shrug. "I'm just...expecting someone."

Mel winked at him, which made Walter feel a bit odd. The train crept past the crossing signal on Concord Road, and he leaned out of the car to scan the small group waiting to get on. The woman with one ear was not among them.

"Mind your step," Mel said as Walter made his way down to the platform, and these words reassured him as always that his welfare was being looked after. He walked slowly across the parking lot, glancing over his shoulder to make sure the woman didn't come running late from one of the station stores. In a few moments, the train took off without her.

Why was he so disappointed? It wasn't a sexual attraction, Walter decided, unless one so subtle that he couldn't discern it. Frankly, he didn't find her particularly attractive. He supposed that in another age she would have been considered a handsome woman. But he disliked handsome women--the blocky faces, the large eyes, the broad cheekbones. To another man, he supposed, she might be considered mysterious, and thereby interesting. But Walter disliked mystery. The simple question, "What if?" could lead to so many disturbing places.

He was obviously not attracted to this woman

sexually, and the evidence was perfectly clear: He had never spoken to her. Surely if he were propelled by a secret fuel of desire he would have managed some small step on the route to intimacy--a brief hello, a smile, perhaps even, "Have a good day." No, not that insulting phrase. Who was he to be using the imperative with this woman? "I *hope* you have a very nice day"--that would be perfectly acceptable. And yet, there were only so many words one could say in passing. She might not hear all of them. She might misconstrue. Better not to risk conversation at the station, but rather, simply stay on board one day in a seat precisely halfway down the car--her customary spot--where the rows turned from facing backward to forward. She would slide into the wide seat without even realizing he was there.

* * * * *

As the second week of the woman's absence stretched on, Walter became worried. His concentration, normally among his strongest attributes at work, failed him several times. At one point, a fellow researcher had the temerity to tap him on the shoulder and ask, "Daydreaming, Walter?" "No," he had replied courteously, "I was thinking." Thinking he certainly was, about why a person would take vacation time at the end of March, known as mud season in these parts. There were other possibilities, of course. She might have fled to some warm-weather island. Perhaps the woman with one ear had simply returned to wherever she had come from, or moved on to someplace new. Perhaps she would never again take the 5:22.

By Thursday Walter had decided to make inquiries, starting with Mel. The conductor knew something about each of his passengers, and it was his habit to share the news, discreetly, up and down the car. For example, with a nod of his head and a few well-chosen words, Mel let it be known to the single women in the car that James, the investment adviser, had just landed a big promotion and was available. On the other hand, Kelly--the young woman with the sad brown eyes--was definitely "not looking and might never be again." She had recently lost her boyfriend of three years as well as her beloved Honda Civic, events that left her crying some days and required Mel to start carrying tissues.

Walter had overheard himself being referred to in a respectful tone as "The Professor...MIT--never married." That wasn't strictly true. He had been hired as a senior researcher to conduct experiments in machine vision, his specialty. It suited Walter to labor among just a few other engineers and their support staff. It suited him even more to retreat each evening to his apartment in the suburbs where he could work uninterrupted on his book of odd designs. He was near finishing his collection of Impossible Objects, such as a teapot with the spout and handle on the same side. It amused him to imagine things that could never work. Often he listened to his short wave, and the crackling sound of far-off voices seemed to him as if coming from a large immigrant family living on the other side of the thin walls. Sometimes, usually before one of his arranged dates, he imagined a woman in his apartment, a wife. What would she be doing right now, he wondered, what would she *do* there?

When Walter, with money in hand, looked up from his seat to ask Mel about the missing woman, he was shocked to see another conductor. "Where to?" the man asked. Mel never talked in such a clipped expression. He always asked, "And where would you be heading?" or "Where can I take you today?"

Walter handed over his three dollars to Edward, as the man's badge read, and said brusquely, "Lincoln."

"Lincoln it is."

"Where's Mel," Walter asked as he peered over the seats, "working up front?"

"Mel? Don't know him."

"He's been the conductor on this line for years."

Edward handed over the ticket. "Well, that explains it then. I've only been the conductor for a day."

"You mean you've replaced Mel?"

Edward shook his head. "I can't say that exactly, not knowing anything about this Mel. I guess he was before my time."

Your time? Walter thought. You've only worked this train for one day. You haven't had "a time" yet. Edward moved through the train. Every few rows Walter heard him say, "Where to?"

There were others besides Mel to ask about the woman with one ear. Several people regularly waited with her at the station to board. Perhaps she had spoken to them. Walter spent the 20-minute ride to Lincoln plotting what he would say in the brief seconds as he got off and the others got on. "Excuse me," he might begin, "I just wanted to ask--do you happen to know anything about the woman with..." He certainly couldn't mention the one ear. "...the woman in the colorful scarves who used to get on here each day?" Walter practiced his question at different speeds and emphases as the train slowed into Lincoln. As he moved down the aisle toward the door, he noticed that no one else was getting off with him, and no one was waiting to get on, either. The Western Local quickly left.

* * * * *

Because March 28 was Good Friday, Walter had no opportunity to continue his inquiry until the following Monday. On that day, he boarded in Cambridge as always, took his seat at the back of the car and waited for the conductor. This time he would be forceful in inquiring about Mel. Then in Lincoln, he would stop in the shops by the station to ask about the woman.

Surely she had made some small purchases there--a newspaper or mints, perhaps even medicine at the pharmacy. She would be remembered.

Edward approached, humming. "Where to?" he asked with not a hint of recognition in his eyes.

"Lincoln," Walter said with a trace in his voice of *You should know that by now. Mel knew the second day.*

"Don't stop at Lincoln." Edward said.

The words and tone confused Walter. Was the conductor offering advice--*Do not stop at Lincoln*, or some new information? "What do you mean?" Walter asked. "The 5 o'clock out of Cambridge always stops in Lincoln."

"I wouldn't know about always," Edward said. "I only know about today. Today this train doesn't stop at Lincoln--the engineer told me himself. Now where else do you want to go?"

"I don't want to go anywhere else. I live in Lincoln. I've been getting off there for two years."

"I can see your problem," Edward said. "That's why people should always ask when they get on where the train's stopping. Saves a lot of this kind of trouble."

The train pulled into Waverly Station, and Edward hurried to attend to the doors. When he returned he said, "Where to?"

Was it some kind of game this strange conductor

was playing? Walter wondered. But Edward didn't appear to be a man capable of sustaining a joke this long. He did appear to be a man capable of stupidity, and so Walter said, "I'll prove the train stops in Lincoln. Let me see a schedule."

Edward checked inside his lapel pocket, but his hand came back empty. "Sorry, all out."

Walter had reached that point his mother had customarily referred to as "her wits' end." He had no wit left, at least to deal with Edward. Walter stood up to appeal to the familiar faces of the Western Local. There were more people than he had ever seen in this car before, but he recognized none of them. Walter sank into his seat. "Just let me off at the next stop-- that's still Concord, isn't it?"

"Of course it is," Edward said taking the three dollars. "That will be another 50 cents."

* * * * *

Walter exited the train at Concord and stood alone on the platform. His Saab was four miles back in Lincoln. There was no cab in sight. A few cars were going by, but he couldn't imagine standing with his thumb out while dressed in a tie and jacket. He would appear ridiculous. He would walk. And since the shortest route between stations was undoubtedly the rail line, he would go by the tracks.

He felt a bit adventurous as he set out. The dwindling daylight did not bother him. He had never been afraid of the dark. He started off briskly, walking between the rails and stretching his stride to land on every other wooden tie. After a while he broke the monotony by balancing on one rail, and he surprised himself by how far he could do it. He looked back frequently, even though he knew he would hear a train coming well before he would need to step aside. At one point he knelt and pressed his head to the cold rail to sense the vibration of an approaching train, but he felt nothing.

* * * * *

The woman gone, Mel gone, the Lincoln stop gone--what else might disappear from his life? Walter descended the long stairway to the platform in Cambridge on Tuesday. Perhaps the train itself wouldn't show up today. Then tomorrow, the whole station would vanish. He laughed at these fanciful ideas. They were more appropriate for some giddy science-fiction story, not the real life of a mechanical engineer.

The train approached on time, and Walter climbed aboard behind a half-dozen strangers. The car was quite full of commuters already. Walter scanned the aisle and finally spotted a vacant seat midway down the car, where the rows turned from facing forward to backward. As he slid into the wide seat, the train pulled away.

"Where can I take you today, my friend?"

Walter practically jumped at the voice. He turned

around, and there was Mel at the end of the car punching out tickets. Walter called to him, but the conductor was busy and did not look up. The train sped on from one station to another, as Mel slowly worked his way closer. When he reached Walter he said, "Hey Professor, how's your book coming?"

"Mel," Walter stammered, "where have you been?"

The old conductor leaned against the seat for a moment. "Oh, just a little safety retraining course they put us through every few years. You know, a train crashes out West and they rush everybody into emergency classes. Why, what did you think?"

"I don't know. You were just...gone."

"That's how the railroad works, they don't give anybody notice." Mel slipped his punch over the green ticket. "Lincoln, I presume."

"Lincoln?" Walter said. "No, I came in from Concord this morning. You don't stop in Lincoln anymore. Didn't they tell you?"

Mel laughed and pulled a paper from his lapel pocket. "Here's the new supply of schedules--just came out today." His big forefinger worked down the row of times and stopped at 5:22. "There it is," he said, "Lincoln."

"But yesterday the train didn't stop there--Edward made me go to Concord."

Mel nodded as if not overly surprised. "The engineer subbing yesterday must have gotten the stops confused. That happens."

The explanation pleased Walter. The train should have stopped in Lincoln. "Well, today I'll have to go to Concord, where my car is."

"Did you ever notice," Mel said as he processed the ticket, "how people always return to where they come from? Wouldn't it be a more interesting world if people sometimes ended up far away from where they set out?"

Walter shook his head, trying to dismiss the crazy thought. But why *did* each day have to be a perfect circle? Why couldn't a person take a sidetrack, go a little ways, and then come back, if need be?

As the train neared Lincoln, a few people got up, and Walter wondered how they knew it would stop there today when he did not. He watched them crossing the parking lot to their cars. As the train moved on, he sensed a person sitting down at the edge of his seat. When he looked over, he saw the woman with one ear.

"I am sorry to intrude," she said, "but the train is so full today."

"No, it's fine, there's plenty of room," Walter said, drawing himself closer to the window so she would not be frightened. He felt the vinyl seat shift under him as she settled into her place and breathed in the intoxicating scent of some delicate perfume. He said, "It's nice to see you again."

She nodded pleasantly and fixed her large shopping bag on the floor between them. The top fell open and he could see a white uniform inside, the kind a nurse might wear. Then her thin hand reached to the knot beneath her chin and began loosening the bright orange scarf. What could she be doing? Walter looked away so as not to be tempted again to stare at the scar. But as he gazed into the train window he saw the reflection of the silk fall from her head. She folded the scarf neatly on her lap.

He turned to her. There on the right side of her head was a perfectly formed, little pink ear. It was smoothly curved at the top and delicately lobed at the bottom. The ear seemed magical to him, as if sewn on by miniature hands.

She tucked a few errant strands of her short black hair behind the ear. He smiled at this gesture, wishing that he had something new and wonderful about himself to show her. She smiled back at him. "Wasn't that your stop?"

He was pleased that she had noticed. He looked through the bleary window at the lights of Lincoln Station receding quickly. "No," he said, "I'm going farther today."

Gentle Breezes

Margaret Grimes--Marge to her Friday night pinochle partners--was not accustomed to seeing death happen. At the moment it did she was reading "The Upper Room" on the davenport of her one-bedroom efficiency unit with the patio curtain closed halfway to keep the afternoon sun from bleaching the upholstery. The Thought of the Day was, "We are drawn to what we focus on." The obviousness of this statement annoyed her. She was beginning to think that much of what religion had to say to her was obvious and why had it taken her all of 79 years to realize that? She looked outside to relieve her eyes for a moment and heard a peculiar sound. Perhaps it was a voice. She couldn't say exactly because she had turned her hearing aid down, which was her habit during the long afternoons when there wasn't much to hear. Shortly after the unusual sound came the strange sight-- something large and dark falling past her sliding door. At first she thought it had dropped out of the sky, like from an airplane. She had heard of that happening somewhere out West.

Marge grabbed her cane and shuffled to the door.

There she saw the fallen thing lying in the snow like an oversized, crumpled-up doll. It was a body. She couldn't say for sure whose, given the angle of the face toward the parking lot. But she suspected it was Haddie, the only one in D Building to wear black knit gloves in mid-afternoon. And, of course, she lived just overhead. It didn't take a genius to guess that the twisted-up limbs belonged to Louise Hadcock Deering.

Marge didn't venture outside to see for herself. First of all, who knew what else might come crashing down from above? Secondly, she didn't much care for Haddie and her yapping Yorkshire Terrier, so she wasn't going to chance tripping over the lip of the sliding door on her account. In fact, she wouldn't have been surprised if Harold or Sam or one of the other men upstairs had tossed Haddie overboard, being fed up at the Yorkie barking all day. It seemed odd to Marge, though, the more she thought about it, because couldn't they just as well have thrown over the dog and let Haddie be?

* * * * *

When the police arrived, they made several assumptions. First, they figured that Haddie had been getting ready to go out because of the gloves. Marge set them straight on that score--Haddie's circulation was so poor she always wore gloves. They also presumed that Haddie was one of the less well-off residents of Gentle

Breezes Estates, given the condition of her under-garments--runs in her stockings, holes in her slip, a frayed brassiere. Marge leaned out of her apartment again when she overheard that crazy notion. "Haddie had money to burn," she said. "Ask anybody."

At this information the sergeant rose from the body and approached the sliding door. "Sounds like you knew the deceased pretty well," he said. "Did she have reason to kill herself?"

Marge thought the question unnecessarily direct. Just then the barking started upstairs, so loud she couldn't hear herself think, and she turned abruptly back inside.

* * * * *

Marge didn't appreciate all the commotion on her patio. She had locked her sliding door and pulled the heavy curtain, but she could still see the shadows coming and going out there. They looked like giant animals. The idea of all those people mushing up her little patch of snow put her in a very uncertain mood as she walked the long corridor from D building to the elevator, rode up one flight and then made her way into C building, past the snack bar and card shop. She didn't even look as she passed the billiards room. She knew Mr. Bennett and Mr. Razelli and that new man in 8D, Mr. Fairmont, with his shirttail always halfway out, were in there leaning on their pool sticks like they knew what they were doing. She had no use for any of them. If you were going to waste time, why not sleep? That was her philosophy.

Marge came upon Audrey Brennan dozing in her motor cart and tried tiptoeing past, but the old woman's eyes popped open. "Mahdge!" she called, "Mahdge Grimes!"

Marge kept her head down. "Can't stop now, Audie. Late for dinner."

Audrey pressed "forward" on the control panel of her cart and it jumped in the way. There was a lawsuit waiting to happen. "You said you'd come by Sunday, Mahdge. I was waiting."

Marge swerved around the cart. "I say a lot of things, Audie. I can't be expected to remember every one of them. And by the way, it's snowing down south."

Audrey's head dropped. She tried hoisting her protruding slip under her dress but just managed to pull both slip and dress above her knees. Marge shook her head at the hopelessness of the situation and tugged them down herself. It was a person's duty to help out the less fortunate, and Audrey certainly qualified as that.

* * * * *

She was late getting to the dining room, and her regular Tuesday night group was waiting for her. She could see them down the hallway at the hostess stand checking their watches, probably talking about her.

Marge didn't like being waited for. She hated being talked about. It made her cross. "You girls could go in on your own," she said from a little distance, shooing them ahead of her.

"That's all right," Florence said, "we don't mind waiting."

"Table for five, ladies?" asked Celia, the hostess when Marge came up.

She shook her head. "We're just four on Tuesdays now," she said, and Celia promptly erased Haddie's little red X on her seating chart. Marge was a little unsettled at how easily a person could be rubbed out. On the other hand, they wouldn't have to endure Haddie's endless prattling any more. That was a blessing.

Marge led her group into the dining room feeling as she always did, like a mother goose followed by a gaggle of little goslings. She could probably lead this bunch into the garbage dump outside and they'd follow her. There wasn't an independent mind among them. She sat in her customary chair at their customary table facing away from the massive silk flower centerpiece in the center of the room. They offended her, fake flowers. Was their some shortage of real flowers she didn't know about? She spread the large linen napkin over her lap and opened the black leather menu. She noted that the featured entrée was meatloaf, which she couldn't abide, having prepared it for her own family for so many years. So on her order sheet she checked off the chicken mignon, with the pearl onions, potatoes au gratin and, of course, baby peas. You could always order chicken at Gentle Breezes.

Dinner proceeded like almost every other on Tuesday night. The scalloped butter reminded Helen of her 30th-anniversary trip to Paris with husband Al, and she recalled their itinerary meal by meal. Sarah lamented that she hadn't done more traveling in her life, but of course she had the four children to raise and trips became just memories while children lasted a lifetime. Florence admitted that she felt blessed having had children *and* travel. Marge chewed and nodded, chewed and nodded, because all of this talking with food in your mouth was just plain bad manners. But something else about the conversation didn't seem quite right to her, and it took till her last scoop of peas to put her finger on it--Haddie wasn't there telling about her children and her trips and her three houses. Could it be, Marge wondered, that she missed the old braggart?

Julie, the waitress, cleared the plates and brought dessert. The others had ordered ice cream. Marge chose the daily fruit, as always, and this time it was grapes, a big pile of them. She held up the bowl for the others to see. "Imagine," she said, "serving loose grapes."

"I wouldn't eat them," Sarah declared from across

the table. "They could have been rolling on the floor in the kitchen."

That seemed silly to Marge. Still, she appreciated the sentiment.

"I can't believe it's almost February," Helen said, dipping her spoon into her chocolate ice cream. "Seems like we just got over Christmas."

"I never saw time go so fast," Florence said digging out a huge helping of raspberry sherbet, and the others agreed with her.

Marge stuck a large, squishy grape into her mouth, and an overwhelming sourness flooded her tongue. It was all she could do not to spit it out. She looked around for Julie, but as always the waitresses were in the kitchen when you needed them. Marge swallowed.

After finishing dessert, the four dinner companions shuffled out to the lobby to claim spots by the large front window where they could see everyone coming and going. Marge sat on the hard edge of the sagging loveseat, trying to get her weight balanced so she didn't fall off the cushion but didn't fall into it either. She couldn't conceive of how the management of Gentle Breezes could be so dim-witted as to buy soft sofas and chairs.

Florence cleared her throat. "Well, it's a shame, I guess we've heard the last from Haddie."

"She was good company," Helen said, "but I can't say I'll miss hearing about her children. What were their names?"

"Rex," Florence said, "that was one of them."

"There was the boy in Arizona--Sam, I think it was," Sarah said.

"And Roscoe," Florence added, "I remember a Roscoe."

Marge slipped her heels out of her dinner shoes. She knew the conversation would soon come around to her--what she saw and what she heard yesterday afternoon. She wasn't about to volunteer the information.

"That woman did go on about her children, didn't she?" Florence asked, and they all concurred, including Marge. Of course, the same could be said of Florence. There wasn't a night went by without her bringing up one or another of her sons.

"Speaking of children," Florence said, "I didn't tell you--my Robert got a promotion. He's second in charge of the whole factory now."

Marge rolled her eyes. She wasn't going to say anything but then she found herself saying, "He's *second* in charge of a factory that makes those little metal things you stick the laces through on shoes? Is there even a name for them?"

"Of course there's a name for them," Florence said. "I'll ask Robert for you when he comes by on Sunday."

"Don't ask on my account," Marge said.

"Oh, no bother," Florence said as she pulled at her

big floral dress to sit right on her. "It's a comfort to have the children nearby. You can see what happens when they're far away like with Haddie--they never visit."

"So," Helen said, leaning forward, "what was it like yesterday?"

Marge pretended not to know what she meant. "What was what like, Helen?"

"With Haddie. Did she really land on her head in the snow?"

"I heard she was naked," Sarah said, "not a stitch on her."

"Except those hideous black gloves," Florence added.

"Well, it was like this," Marge said as Sarah inclined her head so as not to miss a word, "I was sitting on my davenport reading 'The Upper Room'..." Marge went on to recount the unusual noise, her first sight of the body falling, the tell-tale gloves, and of course, the police and all of their ridiculous assumptions.

"I would have fainted away at the blood," Helen said.

"It was gruesome," Marge admitted, "but of course, I was a nurse, so I've seen worse."

"What do you think will happen to that terrier of hers?" Helen asked.

"Don't worry about that mangy thing," Marge said.

"I wouldn't put it past Haddie to leave all her money to a dog."

* * * * *

Wednesday afternoon Marge spent trying to ignore the activity going on in Haddie's apartment overhead. The clomping of shoes was so loud on the ceiling that she wouldn't cross the room for fear the light fixture might shake loose and fall on her. So much commotion over one old lady. Marge certainly didn't want all of this to-do when she went. It was unseemly. Just put her in the ground and be done with it.

At five minutes past four o'clock, she tied her blue silk scarf around her neck and set off for the dining room. She felt a little light-headed at several points along the hall and thought maybe she had forgotten to take her blood pressure pill with her Lasix that morning. She wasn't about to turn around, though. She could get by without her medication for one day.

As Marge moved through the lobby, she gave a little wave to James, the guard, and then peeked into the card shop. She couldn't believe her eyes. "Doris, have you looked at yourself lately?"

The woman behind the counter felt her face. "Why? What's wrong?"

"Looks like you put your lipstick on in an earthquake." Marge held up her hand and shook it to help Doris understand. "No wonder you don't get any customers in here--you scare them half to death looking like that."

Marge left the card shop and started across the lobby. After a few steps a man came running up to her, just about startling her off her feet.

"Mrs. Grimes?"

That was her name. But why was he asking?

"I'm Sgt. Rowley, remember? I talked to you yesterday."

"Of course I remember. What do you think, I'm daft?"

"No, of course not. I'd like to ask you a few more questions."

"I'm heading in to dinner," she said.

"May I join you?"

Marge didn't much like changing her plans at the last minute. On the other hand, she wasn't all that fond of her table partners that evening since all they talked about was Bridge, a game she thought needlessly complicated. And the sergeant did ask in the proper way. "All right," she said, "but I don't know what you can get from me."

* * * * *

Not being a fan of eggplant parmesan, the featured entrée, the sergeant ordered chicken, as Marge suggested. She soon wished she hadn't, for he proceeded to pick up the fried chicken legs and gnaw on them, skin and all. Between bites he asked questions. *Was Haddie depressed lately? What happened to people's units when they died? What if someone couldn't keep up the monthly meal fees?* Marge answered as best she could, but it was a struggle to even look at the detective. Would it have killed him to use his napkin now and then? She picked up her own cloth and dabbed her lips, but he didn't seem to get the message.

"There have been a lot of people dying at the Breezes recently," he said.

"Dropping like flies," Marge said and started down the list: "Haddie, Nathaniel Bergman, Frenchy Larreau, Carolyn Strange, Nicholas Bennett..." She tapped her head to knock the last name out of her memory. "...and Jonas Archibald."

"Do you have any thoughts about all of these deaths?"

Thoughts? Of course she had thoughts. "It *is* an old-age home," she said. "What do you expect to happen here--births?" She knew she was being blunt, but the plain senselessness of his questions was beginning to grate on her.

"The ones you mentioned all happened in the last two weeks. That's more than average certainly."

"Well now," Marge said, "I remember something about that from my schooling. Averages don't mean the same number of a thing happens every period. Some periods you have a lot, others you have none. We just happened to have two weeks with a lot of people passing on."

Sergeant Rowley nodded, and Marge thought that was the end of it. But then he said, "When we talked yesterday, you seemed to think Mrs. Deering was rich."

"She had millions," Marge said.

He shook his head. "Two hundred seventy-two dollars--that's all Mrs. Deering had at the end."

Marge was having trouble understanding. Haddie down to her last few hundred dollars? What about all the houses and vacations she bragged about?

The detective coughed loudly, and Marge leaned out of the way of his germs. "It's probably just coincidence, all of the deaths," he said. "But when there's questionable circumstances, we have to investigate."

Marge didn't see anything questionable about people dying at an old age home, even toppling over a railing, but she held her tongue.

* * * * *

The sergeant left the dining room without eating dessert, and Marge figured he was no wiser after the chicken than before. But she was more confused. Haddie poor? That didn't make sense. Why would someone go to all that trouble to deceive?

Marge departed a few minutes later after her ice cream, and as she passed the elevator it opened and out came Irene Iransky, dressed in her summer robe and slippers. A sad case.

"Irene," Marge said, "you're wandering again."

"I am?" Irene lifted her arm to chew on her sleeve.

"No use doing that," Marge said and tugged the cloth from Irene's mouth. "Why don't you head back up to Personal Care before they call the guards? You don't want them strapping you down, do you?" Of course they wouldn't do that at Gentle Breezes, but Marge didn't see the harm in suggesting they might if it got Irene to turn back into the elevator, which it did.

Marge headed for the lobby. The girls were already there, and her favorite seat was being sat in by Florence. Marge said hello. hovering near the chair.

"Aren't you going to sit?" Florence asked.

Marge squeezed into the only spot free, between Helen and Sarah on the sofa.

"Was that the policeman eating with you?" Helen asked.

"He's a sergeant," Marge said.

Sarah gasped. "Are you a suspect?"

"A suspect? Now how would I be a suspect?"

Florence opened her pocketbook and took out a tissue. "Well," she said, "maybe Haddie took you serious." Marge didn't have any idea what Florence could mean by that and gave her a look. "Don't you remember? At the table last week, you said that if her boys were so all-fired wonderful, how come they didn't visit her?"

Marge thought back, but the furthest she could

remember was counting to 50 brushing her hair that morning. Of course, she could remember sitting on her father's shoulders as President Eisenhower's motorcade rolled though into town, but that was near 70 years ago, not last week. She said, "I don't remember saying any such thing."

"I remember," Helen said. "I thought you were a little harsh."

Marge was getting provoked. Why were the girls remembering her words so darn well when they could barely remember their own from five minutes ago?

"Not everyone is blessed with thoughtful children," Florence said. "That's the sad truth of it."

"Well," Marge said, "I didn't mean it that way."

Helen turned on her. "How did you mean it?"

"I meant she was always going on about them, and it kind of burns you up hearing how good her boys are when they can't even bother to show up. Ten years, not one visit. And they call themselves Christian."

"It *is* inexcusable," Florence said. "I'm just saying you needn't have pointed it out. I think you made her feel badly. And maybe..." Florence opened her pocketbook and took out another tissue. Now she had two in her hand. Marge waited for her to finish her sentence or do something with the tissues.

"Maybe what?"

Florence shrugged and looked knowingly at Sarah, then at Helen. "Well, maybe you pushed her over the edge."

Marge leaned forward, trying to get out of the sofa. "I did no such thing! Why, I was sitting in my own living room when it happened."

Florence rubbed her nose with the tissues. "I meant maybe what you said pushed her over, that's all."

"That's all? You're saying I caused that fool woman's death, that's what you're saying!"

Helen reached out to her, but Marge pulled away. She could see now what was happening here--the three of them ganging up on her. They'd always been jealous of how she dressed and did her hair, and how well she got along with everyone at Gentle Breezes. Marge figured she knew all 272 residents, and they certainly knew her. Could Florence say the same?

"Don't get in an uproar," Florence said. "Nobody else has thrown themselves over the railing after you spoke harsh to them, so I don't expect Haddie did either."

Marge couldn't believe her ears. She couldn't bear hearing another word. She wiggled to get herself forward in the seat, but it was no use. "James!" she called toward the front door, and after a moment, the young guard strolled over, taking his sweet time. "I've seen molasses move faster," she said.

He yawned without covering his mouth. "Need another yank, Mrs. Grimes?"

Marge couldn't believe the stupidity of the question. "No, I'll just stay stuck here all night. Of course I need a yank."

She held out her arms, and James slipped his big black hands behind her elbows and pulled her standing. Marge steadied herself and then took off across the lobby without even a glance back at her so-called friends.

* * * * *

At eight o'clock next morning, Marge filled a washer with her white laundry and headed upstairs to Haddie's. As the organizer of the annual White Elephant Sale, it was her job to go through the apartments of those recently deceased and pick out items that could be sold for the benefit of the Gentle Breezes Aid Fund. It had been a busy two weeks, with all of the dying going on. The White Elephant Sale would be well-stocked this year.

Marge opened Haddie's door and stepped inside. Everywhere there were stacks--of old magazines and dusty books, of blouses and sweaters, of shoeboxes, china plates, linens and Lord knows what else. She wandered through the apartment, picking up things and setting them down again. On her first pass through the living room and bedroom, she didn't find a single item worth taking. The White Elephant Sale had its standards.

Marge needed to get off her feet. She picked up

a picture album from the hard chair near the sliding door and settled in. She figured this was where Haddie sat through the long afternoons, and Marge was surprised at how different the view was from one story up. She opened the album, and there was Haddie as a baby sitting plumply on the ground, her dress spread out around her. Marge flipped through the pages--Haddie with a bow in her hair, Haddie riding a horse, Haddie leaning on a railing on the boardwalk. Then came her wedding picture--Haddie in a beautiful flowing gown and her husband in his Army uniform. He was a small man with a small head and a boy's arms. Marge couldn't conceive of him carrying a heavy rifle let alone taking a whole hill in Italy by himself, as Haddie had described.

Marge turned the page, expecting to see more of Haddie's little war hero, but the photographs suddenly jumped ahead a few decades. In bright color now, Haddie was standing on the porch of a duplex holding a box with three puppies in it. Written underneath was, "My Three Boys--Rex, Sam and Roscoe."

Marge lifted out the picture, thinking that it had been put on the wrong page. But on the back was written the same thing--Rex, Sam, Roscoe. Marge figured that this was a good joke--writing her sons' names on the picture of her dogs.

She turned another page. Haddie was washing one of the dogs in a tub in the yard. The caption said, "Rex

Gets a Bath." Another photograph of a dog sniffing a bush..."Sam Goes Exploring." And a third picture, "Roscoe Begs a Biscuit."

She turned more pages, all of them filled with Haddie and her dogs. Marge remembered her last words to Haddie--*How come your sons don't come visiting, if they're so all-fired wonderful?* What had possessed her to say such a thing? She clapped shut the album and dropped it on the floor. She pushed herself up and looked through the sliding door. She imagined stepping onto the deck, leaning over the railing and letting herself go. How quick and easy it would be.

She had reason, too--who didn't at Gentle Breezes? Did Haddie think she was the only one with great disappointments in her life? *Keep your troubles to yourself*, that was Marge's motto. You didn't hear her complaining about a husband who smoked himself to death before her eyes or two daughters who barely remembered her with useless cards at holidays. Marge had children, so she knew they weren't always the comfort that everyone at Gentle Breezes made them out to be. That's all she had been trying to say to Haddie. That shouldn't drive a person over the railing.

Marge turned from the door. The sight of Haddie's possessions stacked on chairs and tables made her uneasy--a life reduced to such neat, worthless piles. It made her wonder, who would come into her apartment after she was gone and pick up her things and shake their head that so little of it was worth the White Elephant?

* * * * *

Marge ate alone at dinner. She couldn't bear hearing about travel or children one more evening. There had to be more to life than memories. It was below freezing outside for the sixth straight day--how come nobody talked about that? She knew the answer, of course. Only a handful of the residents ever ventured out of the overheated corridors of Gentle Breezes. Why would they care about the cold?

The girls came toward her, gabbing away like clucking hens. Marge stared into her bowl of butter pecan ice cream.

"Did you see Hazel on her way out?" Florence asked. "Wasn't that the sorriest-looking outfit you ever saw?"

Marge had seen Hazel--it was difficult to miss a 200-pound woman wearing a red-checked blouse and a short plaid jacket. Nobody in their right mind dressed like that. Of course, Hazel wasn't in her right mind, so there really was nothing odd about it. "I thought she looked...interesting," Marge said.

"Interesting?" Florence repeated.

Marge ate another spoonful of the butter pecan.

"She must have pulled her clothes out of the Goodwill box," Helen said.

"Maybe she's gone blind in both eyes," Sarah said.

Why, Marge wondered, were they making fun of a poor soul like Hazel? There was a war going on somewhere and the election coming up. Why would they spend their time talking about the crazy get-up of one old woman? "If you can only speak ill of a person," Marge said, "don't speak of her at all."

Florence stared at her in wonderment, as if she'd declared red was green. "What's come over you?"

"I just don't think we need discussing Hazel's outfit."

Florence's face stiffened. "That's just a bit odd coming from someone with a tongue like yours, isn't it?"

Marge pushed away her dish of butter pecan, leaving one big spoonful. She hated Florence's British mannerism of turning into a question what was clearly a statement. She hated even more being surrounded by three old ladies acting as if something were wrong with her. How had it happened? she asked herself as she looked at Sarah's dried-up face and Helen's drooping eyelids and Florence's snow white hair. How had she gotten this old and this unpleasant?

Marge rose to her feet. But where would she go? Back to her apartment to watch Wheel of Fortune and Jeopardy like everyone else? Could she stand one more clicking spin of the wheel? Could she bear going another half hour not knowing the answer to even one of Alex's questions? And what if she managed to keep her eyes open till the 10 o'clock news? Then she'd be treated to murders and rapes and child beatings.

"Don't go off in a huff again," Florence said.

Marge felt faint. She felt as if her bones had no more strength to hold her up. She felt like she might collapse to the floor and never stand again.

"Come on, let's go out and sit awhile."

Florence's stiff fingers fell upon Marge's arm and coaxed her to move. To where--the lobby again to sit like invalids watching people come and go? The thought of it raised the bile in her stomach.

"No," she said, "I'm tired of sitting. I'm tired of talking. I'm tired of being tired."

Florence laughed. "There's nothing you can do about that, is there, dear?"

Marge twisted out of Florence's grip and headed out of the dining room. Folks spoke to her, but she was sick of shouting hello into the ears of folks who wouldn't hear a bomb go off next to them. She walked through the lobby faster than she had in years, straight toward the front door.

"Going somewhere, Mrs. Grimes?"

She turned toward James, who was rising from his seat behind the guard's desk. "Leave me be," she said and wagged her finger at him.

"You know you're not supposed to go out front on your own," he said. "It's icy."

Marge stepped in front of the double doors, and

they opened for her as if she had waved a wand. When she walked outside the sudden burst of cold air took her breath away. She hugged herself with her one free arm, and with her other hand, tapped her cane ahead of her on the black asphalt. The sight thrilled her-- snow plowed up all about the parking lot in mounds so high she couldn't see over them. She felt small again and a little scared at being outside at night.

"Mrs. Grimes?"

Marge turned and saw the guard coming toward her. He was just doing his job, and how could she be angry with him on such a wondrous night? "Look," she said and pointed into the brilliant sky, "so many stars and planets, there must be life up there some- where, there has to be."

James tilted his head back, and Marge thought how sad it was that he probably never came out here either during his shift at the desk to see the world beyond the double doors. She reached into the snow in front of her and pulled out a handful. She squeezed it a little, and her fingers ached from the cold.

"You probably shouldn't do that, Mrs. Grimes," James said.

"I shouldn't?" she said. "Well what if I do this?" She reached back her arm and threw the snowball. It fell to the ground and splattered a few feet in front of him.

James bent over laughing, and when he looked up

Marge was making another snowball. "You're playing with fire, Mrs. G., you know that, don't you?" he said as he reached into the snow bank himself. She threw at him again with better aim, and he danced out of the way. Then he smiled in a way she had never seen him before, as if some mischievous spirit were possessing him. He raised his hand and tossed his snowball in a soft arc toward her. It looked like a beautiful icy comet to Marge, something fallen from heaven. She watched the snowball smack against her stockinged leg, and the shriek she let out was so loud it could be heard all over Gentle Breezes.

The Lake Region Poetry Club

At the age of 74, Gardner Haynes wrote his first poem, which he felt compelled to do by an idle comment on his last day of work at Doerr's, the hardware store in Fosters Corner, Maine.

The 9,500-sq. ft. brick building was something of a landmark in town, sitting as it did atop the only hill. Folks turning off the interstate knew to keep Doerr's on their left to head up to their camps farther north in the Lake Region. To accommodate Gardner's retirement party, Dan Doerr closed down early for a Wednesday, his slowest day. The late afternoon affair was held in the large warehouse behind the store. The shipping boys slid open the huge bay door to let in the low light of April. They hauled out the 15-foot step ladders to string red and green Christmas bunting from the ceiling pipes. They spread a blue Poly Tarp over a 3 by 8 ft. sheet of plywood and laid out the deli spread. In the center they put the large white box containing the mystery cake, donated by Doll's Bakery next door. Their careful work, the boys figured, entitled them to a beer, which they pulled from the 32-gallon Rubbermaid Roughneck filled with ice.

Being underage, they held the bottles along their legs and drank in quick gulps.

Twenty-three people showed up, including Harrison Coyne, the perennial selectman, who brought with him a citation honoring Gardner as "the steadiest of workers in an unsteady world"; and Janette Dureau, the pretty new photographer at Fosters Ledger, who did as Dan suggested and took a few shots of Gardner pointing at the 10-gallon Genie Wet/Dry Vacs with the amazing sale price of $49.95.

The retiring Mr. Haynes politely refused to climb up on the Murray 14.5 Horsepower Tractor, with the snow plow attachment, saying that he had never sold one of those. Janey, as she asked everyone to call her, handed him a SnoForce L-bend shovel instead and coaxed him to "Smile." He obliged and bent over as if using it, which seemed ridiculous to him given that the last of the snow had fallen weeks ago and only an idiot would smile while shoveling.

The assembled crowd leaned against 20-lb bags of Scotts Turf Builder, stacked cross-hatch style like logs. They drank John Courage and Sam Adams beer that Dan had brought back from Boston. Dan freely admitted to his prejudice for beers with first and last names. He passed out the bottles himself, making sure everyone knew he could have gone cheaper and served Bud, but that wouldn't have been right for a gentleman like Gardner Haynes. A few of the younger men found themselves wishing Dan had been his usual cheap self after they tasted the John Courage, which pricked the bitter side of their tongue, and the Sam Adams, which seemed to stick to it.

The employees swapped stories about the stupidest thing they'd ever been asked, such as, "Do you put on the primer before or after the paint?" and "How come this 2" x 4" you sold me isn't 2" x 4"?"

"Gardner," Dan suddenly said, "how many years you worked here?" After a drink of his favorite ale, he clarified himself. "I mean, how many years were you working for old man Jensen before my father bought the place?"

"That would be twenty-two years," Gardner said.

"Twenty-two, plus sixteen with me--that's thirty-eight years. I ain't even lived that long."

Gardner shrugged. What else could he do? It was true that he was old and true that he had sold hardware for almost two score years and it was true that he'd rather be run over by a John Deere than explain how a deadbolt lock worked one more time. It never ceased to amaze him that folks would drive up from the city and bring their fears with them to a place like Maine. This wasn't even Portland where some people actually did get murdered now and then. The only crime around here was the old men relieving themselves in the alleys because they couldn't hold it in until they got home. Once in a while you heard of a fur trap being sprung by a person too lazy to set his own, and some people did get itchy trigger fingers to hunt whitetails before the season commenced. Other than that, Fosters Corner was as quiet as the stars.

Dan tilted his head back and poured Planters Peanuts into his mouth. Through the chewing he said, "You must have heard some stupid questions in your day, Gardner."

The old man looked up from his coffee, which he was holding in his two hands to keep them warm. It could be the dead of August and his hands would still feel stiff and cold, like gloves left out all night in February. He had, Gardner said, but he didn't volunteer exactly what because he didn't feel comfortable making fun at other people's expense. "We're all ignorant," he said, "just about different things."

"That's true enough," said Hector Jones, the garden expert at Doerr's. "My Helen says I'm ignorant when it comes to women, and I told her she's ignorant concerning weeds."

"How about a chair?" Dan offered Gardner and waved to one of the boys to bring him one. "Take the load off."

Gardner declined. Like all Maine men born years ago, he was built on the square and could stand for hours.

* * * * *

As Dan's regular customers dropped in, they sought

out the man of the hour to pump his hand and say their congratulations. Then they went off to see about the spread of sliced turkey and ham with all the sandwich fixings. The talk naturally gravitated to how mud season was near over and the traffic would be starting up again as soon as people opened their camps at Sebago and Highland lakes. It was a mixed blessing, everyone agreed, being on the main route to the water. You couldn't say anything against the money the out-of-staters spent in Fosters Corner on provisions. But some weekends the cars backed up from one end of town to the other, which meant the local folks had to weave through the parking lots and alleys behind the stores to get anywhere. That was annoying.

By 6:30 p.m. Gardner was full, but he felt obligated to try the giant cake with "Fare Well, Old Friend" written on top, because Jacqueline Doll had made it herself and she was handing out the pieces. Jacqueline was older, like him, but not as old as him, he was pretty sure of that. She wore her gray hair pulled back by a rubber band, which he figured was a habit of her profession. When Gardner took the paper plate of cake from her he noticed something else--her thumbs were thick for a woman, probably good for making pie crusts. He wondered whether she had started out with thumbs like that or if years of making pies had developed them that way. His Sarah, he recalled, had very thin fingers.

Jacqueline said Gardner should take the first taste of cake, and everyone cheered when he pronounced it fit for a king, even though he could distinctly taste cinnamon and coconut, which were flavors he liked on their own but had no business being in the same cake, as Sarah would have said. During dessert, he was asked several times in a general way what he was going to do with himself from now on. He answered in an equally general way, "I guess I'll just get to some of the projects around the apartment I've been putting off all these years." The truth was that he had no real plans, but he thought he should appear purposeful. That was a much admired quality at Doerr's.

In actuality, he was retiring because he couldn't stand being around practical objects and practical people for one more day. He figured he had sold enough toggle anchors in his lifetime to hang all the pictures in Portland; enough crabgrass killer to clear the State of Maine of weeds; enough leather-palm Mules to protect every hand in Fosters Corner. He imagined all of the claw hammers he'd sold laid out end to end--they'd reach around the world and probably back to him again.

After the cake was finished, Dan banged his fist on the lid of the galvanized steel trashcan. Everyone quieted down. He hoisted his John Courage and said, "I don't believe there's a man alive more predictable than our Mr. Haynes. When I pulled up to the back-door every morning, he was already there just like he ran the store instead of me. Didn't matter if it was raining or snowing. I thought he might freeze out there if I happened to be late some day, so I gave him a key. He's the only man I ever trusted enough to do that. To Gardner…"

Dan took a swig of beer and everyone else did, too. Gardner didn't know what to do. He couldn't very well drink to himself, even if it was just coffee in his mug. He decided that the proper thing was to nod to Dan for the kind words, even though he wasn't sure being predictable was the highest compliment a person could be paid.

"Speech," one of the stock boys called out, and then a few others did. Fear rose up inside Gardner. He'd never spoken to a group so large before. He'd rather be chopped up in a bark mulcher than talk to more than one person at a time.

"Speech! Speech!"

There was no way getting out of this. He set his coffee on the stack of Quikrete Fast-Setting Concrete and cleared his throat. "Thank you, ah…" Just as he feared, his mind was evaporating. He couldn't even remember his boss' name!

"It's Dan," somebody called out. "You been drinking too much caffeine, Gardner?" Everybody laughed at that.

"Guess I'm a bit nervous," he said and pulled

down on the sleeves of his plaid shirt, which was a habit of his since they had shrunk up from one too many washings. "This place has been my life for a lot of years," he said quietly, and everyone hushed up to hear, "particularly after I lost Sarah. Some of you knew her from when she used to bring my lunch in. Cancer took her early." Gardner stopped and looked at the faces looking back at him. What was he saying? Why on earth was he telling them about his wife and her sickness? He said, "I've never been a man with much to say, you all know that."

"Unless it's about socket sets," yelled out Bull, as everyone called him, the boy who loaded people's trucks.

"Or paint rollers," chimed in someone from the side, and "cotter pins" said another.

Gardner was beginning to get a little depressed. He knew, of course, that he was considered the expert in certain areas, and particular customers were often turned over to him. But hearing his specialties called out like bingo numbers made them seem transient and meaningless.

"I'll miss coming here every day," Gardner said, figuring that's what they wanted to hear since they would all still be coming there every day. "I probably won't know what to do with myself."

That's all he felt like saying, and so he stopped and shrugged to let them know his speech was finished. "Three cheers!" Dan said. "Hip Hip Hurray, Hip Hip..."

The noise got absorbed pretty fast in the big warehouse full of Owens Corning R19 Fiberglas for Attics and Crawl Spaces. People milled around for a little while longer. Hector sliced open a carton of the window boxes that had just come in. He was sure they would be big sellers this season. Dan pulled out his steel tape ruler to measure the empty space by the far wall to see how many Rotary Drop Spreaders they could take into inventory.

Gardner made a point to thank Selectman Coyne for stopping by and told Ms. Doll that her cake was very special. She shook her head quickly. "Not my best effort, really. I guess I shouldn't have experimented."

"No harm in trying something new," Gardner said.

"And what will you be trying new, Mr. Haynes, with all of your free time?"

Her question took him aback. "New?" he repeated, as if it was a word he had to say out loud in order to understand. "Oh, I don't know." He could see she was disappointed in this answer, that she had expected more of him. He pictured himself the next morning walking out on his porch overtop LaZeray's Pharmacy. He saw the Fosters Ledger in his hands and perhaps a pencil for doing the Weekly Crossword Puzzle, which he'd been intending to try. He said, "Maybe I'll just sit on my balcony all day, reading and writing."

"Writing," she said, "that's interesting. What would you be writing?"

He had no idea. There was only old Uncle Ned to send letters to. As for books, Gardner didn't know enough about anything except hardware, and he sure wasn't going to write on that. What was left? "Maybe I'll write poems," he said and kind of laughed.

"Poems," she said, and it struck Gardner that she was repeating the last word of whatever he said, as if his sentences didn't have any meaning to them except for the last word. "Now that would be something new," she said. "I'd very much like to read your first poem, Mr. Haynes."

She put out her hand, and Gardner took it without knowing what to do next. He wasn't accustomed to shaking with a woman. As a matter of fact, he hadn't touched a woman since Sarah. Jacqueline's fingers felt cold and stiff. She cleared her throat, and Gardner became aware that he was staring at their hands clasped together. He cleared his throat, too, and let go.

* * * * *

As Gardner stirred Sarah's special garbage soup in the galley kitchen of his second-floor apartment, he replayed in his mind the party of the night before. Dan had been very kind. A thank you note was in order, for the get-together as well as the 20 percent lifetime discount at the store. That was a generous gift, although Gardner figured he probably had at least one of anything he needed already. Besides, now that he had moved to an apartment there wasn't much for him to fix himself. The guests had all been quite cordial, even Shirley, the cashier, who muttered at him every afternoon when he opened the Aromatic Cedar Closet Lining box to take a whiff. She apparently thought the smell would get all used up.

He sipped the soup and it seemed thin to him, more to Sarah's taste than his. So he rummaged through the cabinets for cans of peas and artichoke hearts to toss in. He stirred for a while and then ate right out of the pot, standing at the sink as he often did after his wife passed on. It befitted him not to make a fuss about dinner.

As the light faded at 7:30, Gardner pulled on the light sweater Sarah had knitted him for just such occasions and sat out on the balcony with his last coffee of the day. The fit of the cardigan was tight, as he liked it. It was as if the threads she had knitted were hugging him.

From this spot he could watch the people come and go at Elvio's Pizza across the street. He could also see the gray stone library sitting back from the road. Near the old oak door, a single bulb lit up the sign saying Municipal Library, Fosters Corner, 1932. It struck him as odd that he couldn't remember ever seeing someone go in there. He wondered if there was a back door off the parking lot. He hadn't set foot in the building himself since dropping off the emergency delivery of Magic Pipe Wrap on his way home from Dan's the night the temperature was going down to 30 degrees below. That was four years ago, he reckoned.

Fact was, he couldn't recall anyone he knew ever saying they were going to the library. At the last town meeting, some folks asked why Fosters Corner needed to spend $1,000 each year on books. Weren't there enough already? Mrs. Sweeney, the librarian, said that was the most ridiculous question she'd ever heard. By that way of thinking the Video Mart should make do with last year's movies. Mrs. Sweeney got her $1,000.

Gardner wondered if any of that money went for poems. As he sat there in that cool spring night with Venus just visible above the spire to the Congregational Church a quarter mile away, he realized he couldn't say exactly what a poem was. Words on a page that rhymed every so often? That didn't seem exactly right, because then nursery rhymes would be poetry and he didn't think they really were. Poems were short, that was a fact, but then he recalled "The Rime of the Ancient Mariner" from his school days. That poem was as long as a book. What it came down to, Gardner supposed, was that a poem was whatever the writer called a poem. He knew Sarah wouldn't have liked the sound of that definition. She was from the old school where words had one certain meaning and one spelling. Saying a poem is whatever the writer says it is--well, that was like saying God is whatever a person says He is. Gardner didn't have a problem with that idea, either, but he wouldn't for the life of him have let on that to Sarah.

* * * * *

The next morning Gardner woke up at 6 a.m. as always, even though he hadn't set the alarm. For breakfast he made buckwheat cakes, which he usually saved for Sunday. He sat at the small circular table long after he was done eating and skimmed through the pile of Fosters Ledgers that he'd been meaning to get to. At 9 a.m. he cleared away his dishes and considered what to do next. In the right corner of his vision, Mrs. Sweeney hobbled up the front walk to the library. Every few feet she stopped to pick up a napkin or cup, the litter that always blew over from Elvio's. Gardner admired her tending to the place, even with her polio right leg, which he knew to be withered under her long brown dress. But who was she cleaning up for?

* * * * *

From the "WPA" carved into the cornerstone, Gardner knew that the Fosters Corner Public Library had been built as a New Deal project. People often remarked how solid the place looked from the outside and marveled that the government had anything to do with it. Of course, that was government years ago.

When Gardner opened the front door, Mrs. Sweeney looked up from her seat behind the desk marked "Circulation." She appeared surprised, and he couldn't be sure if it was because she saw him specifically or just anyone. From just inside the door, he surveyed the main room with its broad oak table in the middle and racks of books extending to the outside, like spokes to a wheel.

"May I help you find something?" she said.

Gardner stepped up to the desk. "Do you have poetry?"

"What was that?" she inquired in a most odd voice, Gardner thought, and he felt embarrassed. Maybe she had misunderstood his accent, since she wasn't from Maine originally, and thought he had asked for pornography.

"Po-e-try," he repeated as distinctly as he could, "like poems."

Mrs. Sweeney swept around the desk and motioned for him to follow. She led him down an aisle, dragging along her bad leg as if it were a nuisance, but no more. She pointed to the stacks. "In the middle is American poetry, on the top, other English-speaking, and on the bottom, everywhere else. Are you interested in any poet in particular?"

Gardner thought for a minute. "There was the one President Reagan liked."

"That would be Robert Service," Mrs. Sweeney said with a nod, "20th Century Canadian." She stretched up on her heels and pulled down a paperback titled "The Best of Robert Service."

"Do I need a card or anything?" he asked.

"To take it out, yes you would, Mr. Haynes, but you can read the book here without a card."

Gardner wasn't surprised that she knew his name--after all, he knew hers. Still, it was strange for someone you had never happened to speak to before to use your name.

"I'd like to take it out...Mrs. Sweeney."

"Well then, we'll just fix you up to do that."

After filling out an address form, Gardner left the library with his first borrowing card and his first book of poems.

* * * * *

When he got home, Gardner pushed his armchair into the rectangle of sun coming through the sliding doors. When he opened "The Best of Robert Service," a bookmark fell into his lap. It said, "Lake Region Poetry Club, Meeting Every Saturday, Fosters Corner Library, Noon." He set the bookmark aside and read through the titles on the contents page until he came to "The Spell of the Yukon." He liked the sound of that. Not that he'd ever been to the Yukon, or anywhere farther north than Aroostook for the potato harvest. But he could imagine a place like the Yukon casting a spell, particularly on a young person.

Gardner turned to page 11 and read:

"I wanted the gold, and I sought it;
I scrabbled and mucked like a slave.
Was it famine or scurvy--I fought it;
I hurled my youth into a grave.
I wanted the gold, and I got it--
Came out with a fortune last fall,
Yet somehow life's not what I thought it,
And somehow the gold isn't all."

Now that was a poem. If Gardner didn't know what poetry was before, he sure did now--"The Spell of the Yukon." There were two more pages of lines to it, but Gardner stopped there. He didn't want to risk ruining what was perfect.

* * * * *

Each day that first week of his retirement, Gardner read another poem by Robert Service. On Friday it was "The Song of the Wage-Slave," which concluded:

"Master, I've done Thy bidding,
and the light is low in the west,
And the long, long shift is over...
Master, I've earned it--Rest."

Gardner understood perfectly well what the writer intended by "master"--a person's boss on earth as well as the One in heaven. He liked the double meaning.

But the more he thought about it, he didn't like the meaning. The poet seemed to be mixing up retiring and dying, which were two things Gardner had an interest in keeping entirely separate.

On Saturday morning he returned the book to Mrs. Sweeney. She thanked him for his promptness and said, "Will you be taking out another poet today?"

"I believe I will," he said. "Do you have a suggestion?"

Mrs. Sweeney thought for a minute, staring at Gardner, as if the answer were inside him rather than herself. "Well, Mr. Haynes," she finally said, "I don't know your political persuasion, of course, but if you're interested in the poetry of presidents, you might like the one who read at John F. Kennedy's inauguration--Robert Frost."

Gardner felt good that he recognized the name and nodded, which moved Mrs. Sweeney to rise from her chair and drag her right leg down the same aisle as before until she found a paperback called "Selected Poems of Robert Frost." *"Two roads diverged in a yellow wood/And sorry I could not travel both..."*

"Excuse me?" Gardner said.

"`The Road Not Taken,'" Mrs. Sweeney said. "Of course, that's his most famous. But my favorite is `The Impulse'--for personal reasons, I must confess."

Gardner assured her that he would read her favorite and left for the short walk home. When he settled into his poetry-reading chair, as he had come to think of it, he turned immediately to "The Impulse." The story surprised him--a bored, childless country woman runs off from her husband without any expla-nation or goodbyes. Gardner wondered whether Mrs. Sweeney, who was known to live with a man who preferred the company of cows to people, was secretly entertaining such thoughts. As Gardner thought about childless wives living in the country, naturally Sarah came to mind. At times she had mentioned her desire to live in Boston, "in her next life," as she always put it. For years she had collected postcards of the city. Would she have moved there in this life if her husband weren't bound to be born, bred and dead in Maine? Gardner could not answer this question. There wasn't much he didn't know about Sarah, but this was some-thing.

He moved on, turning pages quickly until he found a title he liked--"An Old Man's Winter Night":

"All out-of-doors looked darkly in at him
Through the thin frost...
That gathers on the pane in empty rooms."

Gardner knew well that loneliness in dead of win-ter when a person feels the cold on the insides of the windows and wonders how much farther it will come into the room while he is asleep during the long dark night.

* * * * *

As May brought morning to him a little earlier each day, Gardner found himself waking up before 6 a.m. and wondering what poem he would be reading after breakfast. He read each one several times, committing part of it to memory. Then later on, when he was comparing prices at Shaw's Market or sitting in Lou's LaundroMat watching his socks and underwear circling behind the glass door, his mind could go elsewhere, such as to the South with Maya Angelou. He had to admit, he'd been wary of Mrs. Sweeney's suggestion to read the poet Mr. Clinton chose to have recite at his inauguration. Gardner liked to think that it wasn't because she was female, and Black, that he hesitated--but there it was. He couldn't see any way around the fact that he was prejudiced in this matter of poetry. Prejudice didn't sit well with Gardner. So when Mrs. Sweeney stood there in the "20th Century American" stacks holding Maya Angelou in her hands like an odd-colored pup at an animal shelter, he took her.

He tried as hard as he could for the next week to like her writing. The book's title, "Just Give Me a Cool Drink of Water 'fore I Diiie," did appeal to him. Made him think of a dehydrated old man toiling in the fields, accepting all life around him, even if it included death. Such a man wouldn't presume to ask for deliverance from his impending fate, but he might offer as how a cool drink would be nice to ease his way out.

Gardner read the poems "No No No No" and "Remembering" and forgot them immediately. But the opening line of "Mourning Grace" stayed with him--*"If today, I follow death..."* That reminded him of standing over Sarah's open grave, the casket lowered, the people leaving, feeling like he wanted to jump in with her and be gone, too. They had always promised each other to jump in after one of them died, but when the time came, he'd felt foolish even thinking of it.

Each morning that week he made himself his favorite tea, Constant Comment, to sip while reading Maya Angelou, hoping that liking one thing would carry over to liking another. Still, by the time Friday came, he said to himself that he'd been right in thinking her world wasn't his. He came to feel that it wasn't her being a woman or a Black that was the chasm between them, it was how she was so full of herself. He could explain it best in the title of her poem "When I Think About Myself." It seemed to Gardner that's what she was doing all the time. He preferred people who didn't think so much about themselves.

* * * * *

The mail came early that day. Amidst the usual circulars from Shaw's and an invitation from the Congregational women to their Strawberry and Pancake Breakfast, Gardner spotted a postcard. On the front was a loon gliding along in the middle of a large lake, with "Sebago" printed on the bottom. On the back, it said:

"Here I'm Stuck
Wish I Weren't
Here."
  --Uncle Ned

Gardner stared at the card, as if more words might materialize. It seemed to him that this might be poetry. But he remembered a saying around Doerr's: "Give a person a hammer, and he thinks all the world's a nail." Perhaps he was seeing poetry here because he'd been reading so much of it lately.

Gardner counted the words--seven. It seemed to him that there should be more to make it a real poem, but he couldn't say that there had to be any certain number. He thought more about it. If the purpose of poetry was to give out an idea or feeling, then this was a poem all right because it did both. There was no mistaking the message--his uncle didn't like the Sebago Rest Home, even if the back porch did face the lake where the loons called to each other deep in the night.

Gardner got out a sheet of paper from his desk and wrote:

"Dear Uncle, I was sorry to receive your..."

Gardner didn't know what to call it--a poem, a

message?

"...your note. I know it was a big change for you to move in with strangers. But the people don't have to stay strangers. Maybe there's some other men who fought at St. Mihiel like you. Tell them how you almost married that German girl on a bet. You've got a lot of life to share with..."

Gardner stopped in mid-sentence. He looked at his uncle's short scribbled card and his own letter, which was going on and on. They seemed out of balance, like a scale tipped way over to one side. What Uncle Ned had summed up in seven words Gardner didn't feel like he could answer in a whole page. Was that the power of poetry?

He crumpled the letter and tossed it into the trash. On a clean sheet of paper, he wrote:

*"I can't make you
happy where you are,
that's up to you.
But you've always made
the best of things before,
maybe you'll remember how."*

He read his words several times. They seemed to say what he wanted them to, though he wished that the "you" ending the first part rhymed with "how" ending the second. Oh, well.

* * * * *

When Gardner went to the library on Saturday to
return one book and take out another, the oak door
wouldn't open no matter how hard he pulled. He
looked through the window trying to see Mrs. Sweeney, and then he noticed a small paper taped to the
side. It said, "Closed Due to Unavoidable Personal
Matter. Poetry Club Postponed till Tomorrow, Noon.
Sorry for Inconvenience."

A fear ran through Gardner, that the librarian had
followed her impulse and taken off for good. Where
would that leave the library, and him? He perished the
thought from his mind as quickly as it came to him.
He didn't like to be the kind of person who construed
great events in other people's lives as a disruption of
his own.

After he slipped Maya Angelou in the after-hours
book drop, Gardner strolled downtown, since he
didn't have anything better to do with himself. The
day was overcast and spitting rain, which was fine
with him. He didn't mind a little wet. His empty hands
swung awkwardly at his side, as if they didn't have any
good purpose without the expected book of poetry to
carry home.

Just as he was about to turn around at the far edge
of town, Gardner saw the sign for Black Bear Books.
He went in and looked around but couldn't make
head nor tail of what was where. No one asked him if

he needed help. Gardner decided he liked the library better than the bookstore and left without buying anything. Mrs. Sweeney was bound to be back tomorrow, just as the sign said.

* * * * *

She did return the next day. Gardner saw her hurrying up the path at 11:58 a.m., just before opening time on a Sunday. He lingered over lunch to let her get settled, then walked over.

When he opened the library door, Mrs. Sweeney wasn't at her accustomed spot behind the desk. He could hear a voice coming from the annex. Gardner moved in and listened. It was a familiar voice, but he couldn't place it:

*"As grass moves in the wind
waves fall, crash themselves;
sun rises, baby cries
all in the eyes of the Creator."*

"Why Mr. Haynes, I didn't hear you come in."

Gardner spun around and there was Mrs. Sweeney, her arms full of books. "I was just...standing here," he said, which he figured was the honest explanation for what he was doing.

She nodded toward the annex. "I always enjoy reshelving books when I can listen to poetry like that."

"Which poet was the woman reading?"

"She was reading her own self, of course--it's the Lake Region Poetry Club. They usually meet on Saturdays, you know."

Mrs. Sweeney returned to her task, and Gardner found reason to be searching the stacks at the farthest aisle, by the annex. From there it was natural for him to happen to look in. From what he could see, there were four or five women and two men--one young enough to be a college student, the other a carpenter by the name of Bremmer who bought all of his studding at Doerr's. Gardner turned away, but not before Bremmer caught his eye and waved.

* * * * *

When Gardner sat down in his poetry-reading chair that afternoon, he kicked himself for being so stupid--he'd forgotten to check out another book. Now what was he going to do?

He thought of the poem he had heard at the library:

"Sun rises, baby cries
all in the eyes of the Creator."

They were pretty words, and he'd like to hear what came next. But he decided that they weren't extraordinary words--not Robert Frost, that's for sure. In fact, they weren't words Gardner couldn't have written himself.

He took a sheet of paper and pencil from his desk. He stared at the blank sheet for quite a while, but nothing came to him. Writing was harder than he'd figured. He decided just to put down the first thing that crossed his mind...Lobsters.

That seemed like a good start. He knew a lot about lobsters from his days trawling Georges Bank as a younger man, before his hands got too stiff for out-door work. He remembered one particular lobster, a left-hander, that he almost threw back for the wonder-ful bluishness of its color. He erased "Lobsters" and wrote "The Left-Handed Lobster."

Two hours later, Gardner had gone through ten sheets of paper and come up with this:

> *"Left-handed, like me, this lobster crawls*
> *the ocean floor hunting for clams.*
> *Left claw digs and brings them up, right claw*
> *lifts the prey to mouth and cracks it open.*
> *It's a joy to watch a lobster eat.*
> *Pull a lobster fresh from the icy waters,*
> *carry him home squirming to get back to sea.*
> *Drop him in on his back, just a little boiling water,*
> *steam him in his own juices.*
> *It's a joy to catch a lobster.*
> *Clap on the lid*
> *so's he knows he's done for,*
> *Come back in 10 minutes*
> *when the cooking's through.*
> *It's a joy to eat a lobster."*

After he reread his piece for the third time, Gardner added an "m" to "clap," making it "clamp." It was a small change, but it was enough for him to say the poem was done.

Each morning that week when Gardner sat down in his poetry-writing chair, he pulled out a clean sheet of paper, but nothing came to mind. He wondered what Sarah would say seeing him sitting there every day trying to write poetry. "Gardner, what's got into you?" that's what.

His mind filled up with images of her--standing at the stove each morning frying eggs and bacon; bringing him a hot lunch to work at five to noon; at night rubbing his shoulders that ached from reaching to the high shelves at Doerr's. He remembered the way her neck smelled after she soaked in a bath and how she laughed reading the comics each evening. He remembered how much he missed her. He wrote:

THE LOST WIFE
She never liked the cold.
Always sipped warm tea and put on
another sweater.
She never failed to kiss me
goodbye and hello,
even when we argued.
She held my hand in church
and leaned on me

in the market.
I miss her like something
I never figured I could lose.
She wasn't one to complain,
but in the end the pain got so bad
she said, Let me go, Let me go.
The ground was hard to put
her in, the air frozen.
I wished to keep her warm
forever, but I couldn't.
She said, Let me go, Let me go.

* * * * *

When Gardner visited the library on Saturday at half past 11 in the morning, he wore his slicker against the heavy rain that was in the air. In the deep pockets he tucked away his two poems. He felt that they should be close by as he sought out another poet to read.

Mrs. Sweeney greeted him with a smile. "Mr. Haynes," she said, looking up from the box she was slitting open with a penknife, "I've been wondering about you." Gardner was flattered that someone would think about him when he wasn't there. "You left last week without a book," she said. "Have you given up on poetry?"

"No I haven't, Mrs. Sweeney. The truth is that I forgot to check anything out."

She ducked under her desk and came up with three

books. "I saved these for you--I think they might suit your taste."

As Gardner took the books, the front door opened with a bang. Two women came in holding rain hats to their heads and shaking water off their jackets. After a few seconds describing the deluge that had just commenced outside, they headed off to the annex.

Gardner inquired if he could take all three poets--Sandburg, Longfellow and Burns—home with him. Mrs. Sweeney said that indeed he could. Then the door blew in again and with it, a young man with his jacket over his head. He hurried off to the annex. Mrs. Sweeney said, "You'll catch your death of, Mr. Haynes, heading out in a blow like this without a hat. Why don't you sit in for a while till things calm down outside?"

Gardner did just that, sitting in the big easy chair by the window, thumbing through the three books, assessing the poets who would accompany him for the next week. At one point he took out his own poems just to see how they looked side by side to the masters. Every few minutes someone else swept into the library and passed him on the way to the annex. As the church bells rang noon, the door opened and the footsteps stopped right behind his chair.

"Why Mr. Haynes," a woman said, "what a pleasant surprise. I see you're reading poetry."

Gardner turned around and stood up quickly when

he realized it was Jacqueline Doll. Her hair was slick from the rain, and she wasn't fussing about it. He liked that in a woman.

"Yes," he said, "Mrs. Sweeney says if I enjoyed Robert Frost, maybe I'll like one of these."

"I imagine you will," she said. "As I remember, though, you were planning to write your own poetry."

"I guess I did say that." Gardner hoped that this vague reply would lead her to drop the matter.

"Have you, then?" she asked.

There was no way around such a direct question. "I don't know if you could really call it poetry," he said and passed the pages he was holding from one hand to another.

"And you have them with you--wonderful!" she said. "You must come join us." She took him by the arm to the annex where she introduced him as Fosters Corner's newest poet. Gardner nodded to Bremmer, the carpenter, and to a woman he recognized as Mrs. Olper, the church secretary. The others were strangers from surrounding towns.

"We were just going to begin our readings," Mrs. Olper said. "Would you do us the honor of going first, Mr. Haynes?"

Gardner backed toward the door, but Jacqueline closed it with her foot. Now he knew how the lobster felt when the lid got clamped on. He was stewing in his own juices. "I just started writing a few days ago,

I'm not very good."

"Nonsense," Mrs. Olper said, "we don't allow false modesty at the Lake Region Poetry Club."

"Gardner," Jacqueline Doll said to him, and he liked the familiarity of her using his first name, "you did promise to read me your first poem."

He didn't remember making any such promise, and certainly not to a whole club of people. But he was so close to her that he was breathing in her perfume, which was like lilacs, and he couldn't exactly think straight. She took his hand in her strong fingers and led him to the head of the room. Before he knew it he was standing there, his poem in hand, saying, "This is called `The Lost Wife.'" He read:

She never liked the cold.
Always sipped warm tea and put on
another sweater...

Gardner didn't dare look up from the page and see everyone watching him. He read as fast as he could and stumbled over a few words. When he finished with *"Let me go, Let me go,"* he was sure he'd made a terrible mistake writing about something so personal. There was a short silence, and he was about to say, "I told you I wasn't very good," but then they all stood up and clapped for him and shook his hand. Jacqueline said he had natural rhythm. Bremmer remembered Sarah as a fine woman, and the college boy said that poetry was the language of love. It occurred to Gardner in all the commotion that if Sarah were alive to see this, she would fall over dead in disbelief. After they all quieted down, he said, "I have this other poem, too. If you want, I suppose I wouldn't mind reading it."

Jacqueline smiled at him, and Gardner noticed that she wasn't exactly pretty, but perhaps almost-pretty. "One poem at a time," she said, "that's the only rule at the Lake Region Poetry Club." Then she led him by the hand to a seat, which he noticed with some pleasure, was right by hers.

The Dreaming Man

At half past 10 o'clock, Prof. Tyler Curtis climbed the steps of his summer place along the Delaware River, a glass of Cointreau in one hand. With the other he pulled himself up by the railing like a man who couldn't trust his legs to move on their own anymore.

At the top of the staircase he reached inside the bedroom and flipped the wall switch. The light did not come on, and it amused him in a way that he had forgotten again to buy a new bulb on his trip to town. His wife would say that he was absent-minded, but he preferred to believe that he just had better things to think about.

He groped his way into the darkness, feeling along the bed until he reached the nightstand on the opposite side. He turned on the lamp. Along the baseboard, books were piled 10 high, with yellow post-it notes sticking from the pages. On top of the bureau, a dozen wooden animals were lined up from smallest to largest, as if parading obediently into a circus tent. Tyler sipped his drink and looked at these familiar things as a philosopher does, seeking new meanings. About the animals he wondered, why had his wife lined them up by height rather than some more interesting organizing principle?

He went over to the window, pushed up the screen and leaned his head out into the late August night. The moistness of the air dampened his face. He could see the narrow path of the Delaware, but not the water itself. It was as if the river were a black ribbon of gravity from which no light could escape. The professor turned back inside and regarded the books. He had much to read before teaching his new course, "The Philosophical Necessity of Time," at the university in a few weeks. So far he had only prepared his opening remark: "Time is a most useful convention, because it keeps everything from happening all at once." The line was good for a laugh--the students would grant him that much the first day. They might even consider him an eccentric character, dressed in khaki Dockers, sneakers and a Wittgenstein T-shirt under his sports jacket. They would surely be impressed that he had written one of the core texts—"Wittgenstein: The Nearness of Death as Transformation of the Personality."

The illumined numbers of the alarm clock clicked away the last of the hour, shifting from 10:59 to 11:00. It occurred to Tyler that it was somewhat unusual in the digital universe to witness time passing. He felt nostalgic for the analog world of his youth where time swept past in endless silent circles. On digital clocks, life's precious seconds were blurred together as if they didn't matter, bunched up into a much larger minute, then disgorged in a single drop of time that most people never saw. What would be dispensed with next, he wondered--minutes? hours? Perhaps the digital clock of the future would move just once a day, sweep away 24 hours in a short, precise tick.

It was time to sleep. He put his wallet on the bureau as always and undressed to his boxers, tossing his clothes on the armchair by the window. It was a luxury to be careless. It was a relief, in fact, that his wife had gone back early to their apartment in Center City to tend to her garden and cats. The four-poster bed was invitingly spacious without her. He pulled on his nightshirt and climbed in. He arranged himself in his customary way--head face up, arms by his side, a pillow wedged under his knees. The clock clicked away another minute, and soon his breathing became deep and regular.

* * * * *

He was a dreaming man. Sometimes on the weekends he slept in just to dream some more. He couldn't prove it, but he was sure that he dreamed in greater detail than most people and even more vividly here in the country. In this bed, for instance, dreams filled his head each night like an endless reel of movies, starring him. He often wondered about that: Why do people always dream about themselves?

Mist hung over a wide green savannah in early evening. He was standing by a large pit. Flames jumped into the air with sharp, ragged edges, like comic-book fire. One after another animals strode into camp--elephants, giraffes, gazelles and tigers. He understood that they were offering themselves for dinner.

One young tiger stopped at the edge of the dream. He pawed the ground, and Tyler could feel the creature's great hatred of the fire. He was about to charge!

This can't be happening. Tigers don't run toward fire. Tyler knew this implicitly.

The animal kicked up dirt, its paws clawing madly, but came no closer. Tyler relaxed his stance, crossed his arms. There was no danger here.

The man peeking his head in the bedroom window saw the body in bed breathing loud and even. He swung his right leg slowly inside the room, then ducked his whole body through the window. In the dim light coming from the hallway, he could clearly see the professor. His cheeks looked puffy in this reclining position. His chin sagged. His full lips gaped open. It was the face, the stranger decided, of a person who thought too much.

The sleeping figure stirred suddenly, and the man reached for the letter opener on the nightstand. He never carried a knife of his own, of course, and he didn't expect to use this one. Still, he could imagine precipitating circumstances.

He leaned over the bed. The professor's eyeballs were fluttering under their lids. His arms shook at his side, as if strapped there. He was dreaming, but of what? Could he be woken up and asked?

That was a funny thought--rouse a person from sleep, inquire as to what he had been dreaming, and then, by necessity, kill him. It just wasn't done that way. If people heard of it they might think there was a maniac on the loose. Doors would be bolted at night, guns slipped under pillows. The job of a thief would become much harder.

A gust of wind burst into the room, whipping the thin white curtain against the window frame. The man's bare arms shivered a little. A cold front was moving in, as predicted. Why hadn't the professor lowered the window before going to bed? Hadn't he listened to the 10 o'clock forecast? A careful person adjusted his window at bedtime for the temperature that would come, not that was.

The moment of death in the room passed with the wind. The man's hand eased its grip on the knife, and his arm hung limply against his leg. The blade pointed downward, harmless, and that was as it should be. He was a second-story man by trade, not a killer. After all, he didn't hate the man personally--hardly knew him, in fact. He was just another from the city rich enough to rent the Victorians along the river each summer. Putting a knife into such a man's heart would certainly not be a casual act. There needed to be sufficient reason--a sudden awakening, recognition, a weapon. The situation could get messy, particularly if he cut into the wrong place--the thick shoulder, for instance. The professor might scream, perhaps arouse someone walking a dog along the road. Blood could spurt, a frightening possibility these days. Who could tell what vices the professor had succumbed to in his later years? Who could say he wasn't contagious?

The thief emptied the fat wallet of its bills. He couldn't read the denominations, but he expected at least $300, the amount the professor withdrew from his ATM each Monday. Such a loss would be mere inconvenience to him, necessitating another trip into town. He might even blame himself for being careless in misplacing the money.

The stranger left as he had come, through the window onto the porch. He laid the letter opener on the sill where the professor might find it the next day and wonder. An absolutely cautious thief, of course, wouldn't disturb the universe of his victim like this. Inevitably there would remain on the carpet the faint imprints of his shoes--an average size, fortunately--and in the air, linger the scent of a common soap. Otherwise, not a trace.

Stepping out into the mist, the stranger turned up

the collar to his light jacket, and was gone.

* * * * *

At the sound of a car engine starting up somewhere on the road, Prof. Curtis suddenly woke. He sat up in bed and stared through the open window. Gradually his senses came back to him. He remembered where he was and who he was. He recognized the stacks of books on the floor. He saw the animals lined up on the bureau. Next to them lay his wallet. The clock on the nightstand clicked to 12:00.

His cold fingers reached under his nightshirt and felt his heart racing so fast they couldn't distinguish the individual beats. He was terrified, but of what? The tiger charging? What difference would it make if he died in his dream?

The silent wind blew in and chilled him with the hint of autumn approaching. His legs felt heavy. He didn't want to lift himself from the mattress. But his wife had left no blanket at the bottom of the bed to pull over him, and the night would only get colder. The professor got up and lowered the window, just as he should have done before going to bed.

In Memoriam

For most residents of Whitney's Corner, Vermont, the small legal notice placed in the Town Crier came as a surprise: "Attorney Richard Berger will read The Last Will and Testament of Gus and Sarah Sheer at the Arts Hall on Saturday, 2 p.m. prompt. Public invited." What could the Sheer estate have to do with them?

One hundred people turned out, given their natural curiosity and the lack of much else to do on a chilly November day. After the noise of scraping seats and idle comments died down, Attorney Berger dispensed with the legalisms, as was his custom, and got to the heart of the matter: "To our friends and neighbors of Whitney's Corner," he read, "we leave $200,000 for them to do with as the majority sees fit."

The import of this simple sentence was about as clear to everyone as mud in their eye, as Wiley Jones, the undertaker, put it. What were they supposed to do with that much money--support one of the Sheers' pet causes, create a foundation, invest for a rainy day? "Shouldn't be a problem spending $200,000," said Dave Regan, the town's optician, after two hours of discussion, "but that's what it seems to be."

* * * * *

Gus Sheer had died just shy of his 100th birthday, and more than a few people in town suspected it was by his own will rather than physical inevitability. As Dick the barber told his customers, the old guy had probably caught wind of the centennial party planned for him and gotten himself out of attending the only sure way he could think of.

It was a week later that Sarah's 2006 Honda Civic sailed over the rocks by the "Slippery When Wet" sign at the Cliff House Inn. The accident didn't surprise anyone because Sarah was well known for her driving intensity, even at the age of 94.

The temporal juxtaposition of Sarah's tragic accident to Gus's death by seemingly natural causes gave people in Whitney's Corner faith. Everybody always said it would be a shame if God didn't find a way to take the old couple at the same time, and for most folks in town, He came close enough.

* * * * *

The funeral service for Gus was held in the white wood Unitarian Universalist Church on Oneatic Street. The 40-foot bell tower tolled the sad occasion at the unusual time of 5 a.m., out of respect for Gus's being an early riser. A week later, the 41-foot bell tower of the white wood Trinitarian Congregational Church across the road announced the ceremony for Sarah at a more civilized hour, 11 a.m.

About half of Whitney Corner's 472 residents turned up for each service, although not the same half. Everyone in town knew both, of course, since they'd lived there for all of their married life, which was 66 years. But people tended to be drawn much more to one or the other, and to one part of each of them--to Gus's pacifism or uncommon work habits, for instance, or Sarah's militant veganism or intense civic-mindedness.

No one seemed to be drawn to all of either of them, let alone to all of both. In Enneagram terms (a language Sarah often spoke), she was an unabashed 1--a perfectionist and activist who expected no less of others than herself. On the other side of the circle, Gus was a 4--an observer, a plodder, as stubborn a man as ever had been born. By rights they should have repelled each other at first sight. but some fierceness of temperament locked them together year after year. More than one troubled couple in town said, "If those two can stick it out, we can, too."

Most people overlooked the fact that Gus and Sarah lived at opposite ends of their sprawling farmhouse and came together only for the main meals of the day. Some evenings they sat together in their living room listening to the short wave. But they always retired to separate bedrooms, where they couldn't hear each other snore.

* * * * *

Attorney Berger was one of the few to attend both funeral services, which he did in a professional capacity. The Sheers had entrusted their financial matters to him since neither "had the taste for dealing with money," as Sarah put it. He watched Gus lowered to his final rest in Whitney Memorial Park, and then a week later, saw Sarah squeezed in head to head to her husband, since his relatives had gotten into the ground long before her and claimed adjacent plots.

Perhaps because he had resided in Whitney's Corner for only 18 years, Berger came to the reading of the will with a sense of anticipation. It was not often that a lawyer could bring good news. He had figured that townspeople would quickly line up behind one long-standing civic project or another--beautifying the Town Common, came to mind, or expanding the library.

But the first question from the floor indicated otherwise. "I was wondering, just for wondering's sake," Will Mahoney thought out loud, "the majority could vote to divide the money among everybody living in town--is that so?"

"That would be up to you," Berger said. It was not for him to judge what use was right or wrong.

"How much would it end up being, per person, that is?"

The attorney took out his calculator and punched

in some numbers. "Rounded off, about $430, for every man, woman and child."

A few whistles echoed across the hall. "I could buy a new refrigerator with that," Anne Klein said. "Don't seem fair, though," Sam Gash countered. "A big family like yours gets a lot more."

J.J. Hunneman had the biggest family in town--two grandparents, a wife, a sister, five children and himself--10 people living under one roof. It was easy figuring to see that he'd stand to make $4,300. J.J. stood up. "I'd have the most to gain from dividing the money, but I don't see that that's why Gus and Sarah left it to us."

He sat down without elaborating, which prompted Roger Doans to ask, "Why didn't they just tell us what to do with the money?"

"It wasn't their way to give with strings attached," Berger said. He cited the very hall they were sitting in--the Sheers had put up half the money toward its construction but refused to have the building named after them or have any say in its design.

Everyone nodded at this perfect example of philanthropy. But Roger remembered an earlier donation of $10,000 that Sarah had made to the regional high school over in Carver where she taught for 30 years. That time she spelled out exactly what the money could be used for (arts materials, dramatic productions, visiting writers) and what it could not (organized sports, computers, administrative over-head). Walter Payne, the fireman, said the conditions were understandable in that case because the school couldn't be counted on to make the proper choices. "Gus and Sarah trust us," he said, "and I think we can do them right, if we let their lives be our guide." The meeting adjourned just before nightfall. It was apparent to everyone that they needed more time to decide how to spend this unexpected gift.

* * * * *

One week later, more than 200 people filled the Arts Hall. Upon reflection, Berger realized that it had probably been a bad idea to start with a "social hour" in the annex. People who were only cordial enough to nod at each other in town were now elbow to elbow, sipping glasses of Don Boyd's freshly squeezed apple cider. Voices rose more than once as one person or another took issue with some interpretation of Gus's or Sarah's life. No one objected when Berger ended the social hour fifteen minutes early.

The assembly naturally divided into friends of Sarah on the left, and Gus on the right. Berger set up a microphone in the center aisle, and a dozen people immediately lined up. Daniel Langford, now the oldest person living in town, was allowed to speak first, given his inability to stand for more than a few minutes at a time. He started his speech, "I've known Sarah and Gus for going on 50 years," and thereafter, everyone else followed his rhetorical lead. Nobody wanted to be the first one to refer to them in the past tense.

The loyalty of the speaker became immediately apparent by which of the couple was mentioned first. Surprisingly perhaps, more women seemed to speak up for Gus. Lynn Bacon recalled his jailing and torture at Leavenworth for being a conscientious objector to World War I and recommended establishing a Center for Peace and Justice in his name.

A few veterans shook their heads at a man refusing to serve his country. Lyle remembered that Sarah volunteered as a nurse in that war and was a militant defender of democracy. She founded the local chapter of League of Women Voters and was known to patrol Main Street on election day asking people if they had voted yet, and if not, when they were planning to.

Janet Humphrey, former president of the League, suggested that some of the money should go toward voter education. But Charlie Apt recalled Gus saying how he'd been betrayed in `16 by Woodrow Wilson's campaign slogan, "He Kept Us Out of War," and wouldn't ever vote again.

Ana Sepanian asked what would happen to Rocky Farm now? Where would people go to learn about Gus or Sarah's ideas? Most visitors to the farmhouse stayed just a few hours, but others ended up there the whole growing season. They were drawn by the books--Gus's autobiography, titled "Tortured Memories," and Sarah's scathing attack on modern education, which she called "Rotten Schools."

And then there were the animals to think of, Ana said. Any stray found within 20 miles was invariably brought to the Sheers. They took in irritable llamas, broken-down greyhounds, a coyote whose paw had been mangled in a trap, a three-legged fox, and untold numbers of dogs and cats. Occasionally the stray was a runaway teenager, which the Sheers found to be the hardest animal to patch up and send back into the world. They were known as rescuers, although they didn't like to think of themselves that way. Most creatures can rescue themselves, Sarah said, if you just get them over the rough spot.

From the side of the Arts Hall, Rev. Shoneforth from the Trinitarian took over the floor without the aid of the microphone. In his deep baritone, he said that the legacy of Rocky Farm was absolute reverence for all life. But Dave Fried, the carpenter, interrupted with apologies, because that wasn't completely true. He remembered the summer before seeing Sarah jabbing at an English sparrow that had invaded her bluebird box. Would have killed it, too, Dave said, if he hadn't intervened.

Someone wondered out loud what Gus would have done in that situation. The general opinion was that he would have let the sparrow be and built another home for the bluebirds.

Dick the barber proposed starting a foundation called "The Foundation for a Better Tomorrow." That seemed vague enough for most people, but Joe Warren pointed out that Gus didn't believe in tomorrow. He ascribed to the Greek view that things either took place now, or not now--forget about the past or future. He kept no calendar for appointments. Callers were told to just show up and he'd see them if he wasn't busy. Most of the time he was busy, because he did things the old way, like clearing pasture by hand. After sawing down a tree, he'd sort the pieces--the trunk for firewood, large branches for poles and stakes, the small branches for pea supports. Nothing was thrown away.

Without either Gus or Sarah in attendance, their friends continued through the afternoon to create whole belief systems out of remembered comments. "Never have anything to do with unearned income," someone quoted Gus to undermine the suggestion that the $200,000 be used as an endowment for the town. "But in their later years, both of them lived off their investments," another countered. Even Sarah's lifelong commitment to vegetarianism was challenged by Jill Mahoney, Will's wife, and proprietor of Mahoney's Dairy Bar. She said that once a month Sarah ordered a few gallons of Neapolitan delivered to their home. The reaction from Sarah's side of the hall was disbelief. But Rev. Shoneforth acknowledged what Sarah had confided to him: If she had her life to do over, she would have climbed more mountains and eaten more ice cream.

About 4 o'clock, the adults had had their say and Eileen Robinson's little girl, Lila, stood up to recount the day Mrs. Sheer caught her picking a wildflower on Red Mill Road. "She pointed at the spot where I picked it and said that now there wasn't anything beautiful there for anyone else to see. She said that only selfish little girls pick flowers."

Friends of Sarah cheered this story, which clearly showed her teaching instinct at work and her philosophy that it takes a village to raise a child. When the clapping died down, mechanic Ron Smith, who labored to keep Sarah's old Civic in running shape, said a little too loudly, "Why couldn't the old sourpuss have just let the girl enjoy her flower?"

The words hung in the air like a puff of foul smoke. Janey Shuman, Sarah's dental hygienist, couldn't let the insult go unanswered. "Sourpuss?" she asked as she rose to her feet. "If you want sour, you had no further to look than Gus Sheer. Did that man ever laugh in his life?"

Ron wiped across his mouth with his sleeve, a suggestion his wife had made to keep him from saying anything rash. But when he took his hand away he couldn't help saying, "I wouldn't have laughed either, married to that woman."

Janey stormed into the aisle and poured her glass of ice water over Ron's head. He leaped out of his seat and knocked over the microphone, which banged so loudly on the floor that Lila Robinson dropped her cup of cider. As the brown stain seeped into the new white carpet of the Arts Hall, everybody pressed toward the center to see.

"This is what it's come to?" Rev. Shoneforth said as he rose from his chair, "harsh words and precipitous acts? What has money done to us?"

The reverend frequently spoke in questions like this, to the annoyance of most Unitarians, who preferred a minister to flat out state his opinion, not dance around the subject. "Sit down, preacher," the call came from Gus's side of the hall, "we don't need a sermon on a Saturday." From the back seats a paper airplane came sailing overhead and smacked the reverend in the chest.

Faces grew red with anger. A few fists shook the air. Richard Berger adjourned the meeting.

* * * * *

In the following weeks, Whitney Corner's only attorney was stopped a number of times on the street and asked when he would convene another meeting to straighten out this money mess. He told them never. As executor of the will, he'd come up with his own settlement and let them know. He announced his decision in the Whitney Crier--$100,000 would go to

Gus's Unitarian, and $100,000 to Sarah's Trinitarian, to do with as the congregations saw fit.

The Unitarians immediately sought bids to repair their bell tower, which was in need of shoring up. In the specifications, they inserted a sentence raising the height by two feet. When the Trinitarians saw the scaffolding go up across the street, they waited with their money in the bank to see just how high that bell tower would rise.

The Last Meal

From his dining room window, J. Quinn Brown saw the cardinal perched in the scrub bushes at the edge of the yard, a splash of red on a white canvas. The light snow had stopped, and the sun was shining fiercely. It was near 10 o'clock. The bird knew it was time to be fed. Past time, actually.

The old man felt guilty because the thought had crossed his mind that maybe the cardinal wouldn't show up this morning. It was more than a thought--a hope, in fact. The truth was, Quinn felt a bit more tired than usual. There wasn't anything particular he could point to. If it were his high blood pressure, he knew his face would be flushed. If it were his blood sugar, he'd be dizzy. He was just feeling tired. Maybe he shouldn't have had the three eggs, but that was done with and there was no use worrying about it.

Quinn looked outside. The cardinal seemed to be looking in, his head cocking at all different angles, expecting to be fed. Expectations, Quinn said to himself as he pushed his chair away from the table, can be annoying, especially when they're somebody else's. He'd found out that more than once in his 78 years.

For example, just because he'd gone all his life without liquor passing his lips, people had come to count on him that it never would. They'd drink themselves, of course, and then toast him like he was St. Abstinence.

You might have thought he'd set fire to the Bible the way his children were shocked to see him sip champagne at the wedding of his oldest grandchild two years back. He found the taste sharp on his tongue, and he kind of liked that. There wasn't much he could really taste anymore, so it was a pleasure to discover that at least one part of his body hadn't lost its senses altogether. But when he lifted that glass to his lips again, one daughter or the other had reached in and taken it away, saying he "better not." He hated that expression. He'd been hearing it far too often after his minor heart event. "Better not"--the words didn't even make sense. And what calamity could possibly befall him sipping champagne?

He braced himself on the table to stand up, and he could hear his knees cracking a little. That made him wonder--how could he hear such a faint sound when he couldn't hear talking over the phone? The girls were always hounding him to get one of those Miracle Ears they'd seen on television. Shirley, his oldest, had gone so far as invite the salesman out as her 75th birthday present. Imagine blowing out the candles on your cake and then having some stranger poking around your ears. Quinn was proud of himself for keeping his tongue that day. He'd learned you can't argue with young people. But it would certainly take a miracle before he'd stuff one of those gadgets in his ear. They made you hear too well, and it was darn near impossible to separate all of the words. Why in the world would a person want to hear everything? He'd spent enough of his years purposely ignoring the silly talk around him. Now he had a perfectly good excuse for not listening, and he wasn't about to give it up.

Quinn pulled his overcoat off the hook inside the door to the garage. Then he walked past the Dodge Ram 1500 that he wasn't allowed to drive anymore. The girls had wanted to sell it for him. He told them no, he didn't need the money, and he did need the illusion that he could still drive, which is what the truck meant to him. "At least leave an old man his illusions," he said to them. "What else do I have left?" They gave in so quickly that Quinn realized he had a powerful argument he could use about other things, if he didn't use it too often.

On warm days he started up the Ram, and it thrilled him to feel the power of the engine running through his body. He didn't tell his daughters that sometimes he backed the truck out to the street, drove it down to the end of the cul de sac, then back again. It felt like a trip to Mars

Quinn pushed the button now to open the garage door and picked up the half-full bag of cracked corn in his good right arm. He stepped into the morning, and the air felt fresh on his face. It was warmer than he expected. He'd noticed lately that weathermen were always making the outdoors seem harsher than it really was--the snow deeper, the temperature colder, the wind stronger. How many times had he heard one of them warn of dangerous wind chills that could freeze your skin in a few minutes? Never happened to him, and he went out to feed the birds every day of the year. It seemed to Quinn that those weathermen were just trying to make themselves more important by being the messengers of doom.

He liked the cold. The colder the better. He didn't like all those folks who run out to the market every time the forecast predicted a foot of snow like it was the end of the world barreling down on them. He saw them on the TV news carrying bags full of bread and milk and eggs. "Stocking up," they'd tell the report-ers. "You can't tell how long we might be snowed in." From the way they talked Quinn could tell that most of them had been born elsewhere, which meant they'd actually chosen to live in New England. What were they expecting coming here if it weren't a little winter?

He walked up the back steps to the yard, holding tight to the railing. He stepped gingerly onto the snow and felt the icy crust underneath an inch of powder.

He knew that if he put his weight on his heels he could punch into the crust and walk without slipping.

At the edge of the yard, in the scrub bushes, the cardinal waited. Quinn made his way through the snow. Nearing the feeder he lifted his foot and a noise from behind surprised him. His head turned a bit. Used to be it was Emma tapping at the window for him. She'd been gone four years now, and still Quinn expected her to be waving at him from the living room to be careful.

He turned forward again. His boot hit the snow flat, and the icy crust didn't give under his weight. His right leg slipped out from under him. His right arm, weighed down as it was by 10 pounds of corn, was useless to steady himself.

He knew he was falling and there was nothing he could do about it. He thought about that obnoxious commercial--"I've fallen and I can't get up!" Such condescension--reducing a frail old person to the whimperings of a six year old. Why couldn't they have just said, "I've fallen"? Why give the world one more phrase to ridicule old people?

He felt his legs splaying out like a wooden marionette. He visualized himself a few seconds later spread out on the snow. Would his lips fall back by some strange incline of his body and freeze a silly smile to his face? Is that how he would be found? Would he look like some misused puppet, left in a heap because the legs and wires couldn't be untangled?

He dropped the bag of seed. His hands flapped in the air. He felt like an injured bird still holding on to the hope that he could fly again. He was falling, and he knew it. The seed bag smacked into the crust of snow and spilled down the slope toward the feeder. Quinn hit the snow head first.

* * * * *

The bright red cardinal sitting amidst the bushes waited for a few minutes until the commotion in the yard was stilled. His head twitched as he tried to make sense of the body spread out over the snow, and the streak of red dripping onto the cold whiteness of the yard.

The bird took off in an arc and landed delicately near the cracked corn. His head twisted side to side, watching for crows or the black cat that liked to sneak up from behind the maple. The bird pecked at a ker-nel, then flew back to its bush. He was in luck. The mourning doves were off in another yard, and the crows seemed scared off by something. The cardinal saw that he was alone to feast. He swooped over the yard again and settled amidst the thickest covering of cracked corn he had even seen.

The bird ate like a creature unsure where its next meal would come from.

Part Two

Stories in which....

A connoisseur of marijuana scrambles for supply and ends up an unexpected hero;

A mother sits through the trial of her son, praying for an outcome they both can live with;

A visitor to the mall can't help seeing everything going on, but what does he miss?

An unusual man with unusual convictions has a hard time finding love;

A worker in a mental institution struggles to hold onto her own sanity;

A young woman wonders if this will be her first visit to her boyfriend in prison or her last;

Death takes center stage in a show everyone is watching; and

In the first chapter of the novel *Blue Hour*, a baby is found in an unusual place.

Xavier and the Eye of Knowledge

Xavier Terrence DeSault was at that annoying time of life between sources. His regular guy was temporarily closed for business, being penned up for three to six. The dude taking over for him had just moved to town and was having trouble getting supply. Xavier was left to hustle for himself on the street, which he didn't like at all. You never knew what was getting dumped on you.

So when he left the Salvation Army Utilities Help Office, he thought God must be looking out for him because there was Bobby D. walking past, dressed as always in a flannel shirt, jeans and boots, like some fucking country singer. They weren't friends exactly, more like guys who didn't like each other. Still.

"Hey, Bobbo, my man," Xavier said, "how you doing?"

Bobby D. slowed down, a good sign. "I'm doing."

Xavier fell in step alongside him. "No wheels?"

Bobby D. shot him a look like *don't ask.*

"You hear about Joey?" Xavier said. Joey always made a good story. "He flipped out in Shaws hitting on some super-charged weed, water-water, you know?" Bobby D. didn't seem to, so Xavier kept on. "Chicago shit dipped in formaldehyde. Nasty stuff. I wouldn't have it pumped in me when I'm dead." He made a fist and rubbed the thick blue artery popping up on his arm.

Bobby D. picked up his pace, zipping around people on the sidewalk. Xavier kept up, a step behind.

"So Joey was walking down the aisles at Shaw's talking backwards, not even English, like Italian or some shit. *Backwards Italian.* So the guard comes to take him out and Joey grabs these bottles of oil and vinegar and says `Stand back!' The guard thinks he's going to throw them, right? But you know Joey when he's blazed." Bobby D. ducked left around this raggedy old guy with an armful of clothes. Xavier dipped left himself, shuffled a little, a football move, catching up again. Something else popped into his mind, another Joey story. "Remember that fucking huge parking lot at Arsenal he climbed on the wall saying he could fly and then bang, he jumps? I thought he was dead lying on the cement all twisted up, like a fucking huge pretzel. The tree broke his fall, but he won't admit it. He really thinks he was flying."

"So," Bobby D. said after a drag on his cigarette, "Joey was in Shaws...?"

"Yeah, you won't fucking believe it, he poured the oil and vinegar over his head. Five bottles of it, like he was a fucking salad. That dude is out of his mind."

Bobby D. looked over like he didn't believe it. "I swear," Xavier said, "I heard it from Tico."

"Yeah, whatever."

That surprised Xavier. Everybody believed Tico. Enough of the fucking small talk. "So, like, you got anybody in town now?" Xavier said it smooth and light, just asking.

Bobby D. laughed. "Last time I saw you was outside Liquorama, remember? I asked you for a hit. You waved me off, man, waved me off."

Xavier scratched his neck. "I did that?"

"Yeah. You."

"That was wrong. I was out of it, you know. That wasn't me. I always give you shit. You're my…" What was the word? There had to be one, but Xavier couldn't come up with it.

"Yeah, that's me," Bobby D. said as they reached the corner, "your *whatever*." He stopped for a moment, seemed to be thinking, had that look. Xavier knew his mouth got him in trouble, so why not keep it shut for once? They hung there waiting for cars to go by like fucking law-abiding pedestrians. Felt stupid, not something Xavier wanted to make a habit of.

"Guess it wouldn't hurt bringing business with me," Bobby D. said when the light changed. He stepped off the curb. "You got money?"

Xavier followed. When they reached the other side, he pulled out a fistful, mostly singles, but it looked good.

"The guy lives a block over," Bobby D. said. "He's got killer bud, never lets you down. He's my only guy now, so don't fuck with him."

Xavier licked his lips. What were the chances, killer bud just around the corner?

* * * *

He was a spooky dude, Q, dressed in black, head to toe. And the whitest face you ever saw. The Michelin rubber man had more color.

Xavier was ready to lay out his money, grab the weed and run, but Q. insisted on lighting up a sample, try before you buy, his policy. No arguments later. They left Bobby D. on the porch smoking Basics one after the other and went inside the apartment, through the kitchen into another room with a mattress, couch, dresser and nothing else. Couldn't be doing much business, Xavier thought, living like this. Q. told him to sit, then lifted a fat orange cat off the mattress and set it next to him. It was the strangest creature Xavier ever saw, shaved to the skin except for a thick mane and a tuft of hair at the end of its tail. A miniature lion.

"Be right back," Q. said.

The thing stared at Xavier with bright green eyes, like in one of those sci-fi flicks, a devil cat. He leaned off the couch, tried to see in the kitchen, what the guy was doing. The cat meowed or hissed, kind of both at the same time. "Good fucking kitty," Xavier said, reaching out one finger, figuring he wouldn't chance getting his whole hand clawed up. The cat sniffed, then backed away a little and settled down. When Xavier looked up, there was Q. filling the doorway, a bag in his hand.

Xavier jumped up, putting a little distance between himself and the cat. "So, what's the deal?"

"Chronic?" Q. said.

The devil-cat looked up, seemed to shrug, Xavier thought, then jumped off the couch and trotted back to the mattress. King of the place.

"Okay," Q. said, "let's go outside."

The porch was slanted so you'd slide off if the railing wasn't there, fall two stories, crack your head open. There was one rusting metal chair and a plastic table slit through in the center, like from an ax. Q. handed over a joint. Xavier looked around. A million windows. Somebody could be watching from any of them. One of those Minuteman dudes with a rifle, ridding the neighborhood of bad influences. But Q. didn't seem worried. Or Bobby D. leaning against the railing, lighting up another Basic.

So Xavier took a hit, let the smoke sink into his lungs, then put the joint to his mouth for another quick toke, doubling up, his usual way. He offered the joint to Q., the right thing to do, but the guy shook it off. Was Bobby D. setting him up, cops with binoculars in the neighbor's house? Xavier took another drag out there on the rotting old porch with Bobby D. sitting on the railing now, earplugs in, his head bobbing, lips moving, nothing coming out. The Michelin Man was talking his face off about the JFK assassination, the fake moon walk, all that old-time shit.

"The Masons, you know them?" Q. asked directly, no getting away from the question.

Xavier knew a few masons. Fucking hard work lifting rocks all day.

"The founders of the country were Masons--Franklin, Washington, Jefferson, the guys who wrote the Constitution. They ran everything in the beginning and fixed the system to work for them."

Xavier coughed a little, the smoke scratching his throat. That was embarrassing, like some rookie puffer. He pictured his mason-friend Max with a shit-eating grin on his face writing the Constitution..."First law: Everybody must get blazed!"

"If you don't believe me," Q. said, "look at your money."

"Huh?"

"You have a single?"

"Yeah."

"Pull it out."

Xavier did, no big deal, a singleton. Q. took it from him and turned it over. "See this eye on the top of the pyramid? What's that doing there?"

Xavier shrugged.

"That's the Mason symbol, the Eye of Knowledge. It means they're watching. Every single time you buy something, they're watching."

Xavier took another puff. "That's some crazy-ass shit," he said to keep Q. talking, because as long as he did, the weed was on the house. He could get a free high out of this.

"The Masons run the world," Q. said, staring hard at Xavier now. "Banking, finance, commerce, government. But maybe you don't see it that way."

"Huh?" Xavier said again. It was the most frequent word in his vocabulary.

"What do *you* think?"

Not many people asked him this question. His friends knew better. Not a single thought came to his mind. Fact was, he really didn't give a fuck. The assassinations, the conspiracies, the wars, the Masons--they didn't affect him one little bit. He didn't care who ran the world as long as they didn't try to run him. So what if his teachers and parents and politicians lied to him all his life? He figured everyone was lying, and it didn't matter since he was lying too and not listening to anybody anyway.

Q. reached for the joint--the freebie was over.

"Good shit," Xavier said as he handed it back. "A gram for 15, right?"

"An eighth for 35," Q. said, pulling the bag from

his pocket. "First-time buyer's deal. Full price next time, no negotiations, no cuffing."

The numbers floated through Xavier's head. He could sell two grams for 15 each, keep the other gram and a half for himself. He'd only be out 5 bucks. This shit practically paid for itself. You couldn't afford not to smoke. But the deal seemed too good to be true. Was he being suckered in with good weed then dumped with schwag? He stared at the bag in Q.'s hand but couldn't tell. He had to ask, get the guy on record. "This stuff ain't cut, right?"

Q. got this angry face on him and pulled the bag back. "How would I cut it? This ain't coke, man. Respect the weed."

He looked over at Bobby D., who took off his head-phones.

"What?"

"Your buddy thinks I'm dumping schwag on him."

"Fucking eh, Xavier," Bobby D. said, "I told you not to mess up. My man sells really good shit, and nobody sells lower."

Q. was already tucking away the bag, like taking his toys and going home. A touchy sort.

"I didn't mean nothing," Xavier said. "I'll take it, the eighth."

Q. considered a moment, then tossed over the bag. Xavier tucked it in his back pocket. He took out his money, a twenty, a ten, and then five ones with that weird eye staring up at him.

"Fucking masons," Xavier said and handed over the bills.

* * * * *

He got used to Q., doing things his way. Parking up the street, coming in the back, talking all that paranoid shit like he believed it. Went off no problem for a few weeks, swinging by Q.'s around 4 pm, just enough time to meet his buddies in the park behind Liquorama 420 every Friday afternoon. He didn't care much about time, never wore a watch, but 420 was 420, the time to blaze.

The thing was, he was usually late, and that didn't look good, like he wasn't respecting 420. So he got the idea Thursday night to swing over to Q.'s and make his buy, planning ahead and all that shit. He should have known that wouldn't turn out good. It became a fucked-up situation, and what disgusted him most was the way it ended up making him look like a doll, of all things. That's what Cindy called him--a perfect *doll*. In front of his Liquorama buddies, too. She threw her arm around his shoulder and sucked on his neck until it drove him crazy. Then she pulled away and said, "He's a doll, isn't he?"

No he wasn't. Sure, on the way back from Q.'s something got into him and he ran into a burning house to save a little girl while her father--the actual father, not some step-guy or fake foster dad--stood outside in his boxers screaming for help. It was sickening, a dude crying like that with his old lady yelling "Do something, do something!" Xavier knew what to do. He pulled his hood over his head and yanked his sleeves down over his hands and pushed in the front door.

The sudden blast of heat knocked him to his knees. That made him angry. It was personal now. Xavier vs. The Fire.

Round One, the fire knocks Xavier to the floor, singeing his eyebrows.

Round Two, Xavier gets up coughing and squinting, his eyes blinded by a light fiercer than a tanning booth. He touches something metal, and it burns his right hand like acid from a leaking battery.

Round Three, the fire nips at Xavier's jeans. He feels the flames crawling into his pocket. *This isn't good, $40 worth of smoke going up in...smoke! Somebody would have to pay for that.*

Round Four, he pats down his pocket and hears a whimper near his feet, like from a dog. He bends over and feels hair. His fingers grip into it and lift.

Round Five, the thing squirms in his arms and he squeezes to hold it still. He spins around but can't see which way's out. It occurs to him that he, Xavier Terrence DeSault, could die there, burnt to ashes. They'd probably run some sort of test on him and find out that he has more weed than blood running through his veins. They'd figure he was responsible. As far as he could remember, he wasn't.

Round Six, Xavier needs some serious help here. He shouts out a prayer, "Jesus Mary Joseph get me out of this fucking hell!" One of them does--he doesn't care which--opens doors just like his mother always said, and Xavier walks through into the sudden cool air. Now it's the dark that overwhelms his eyes. He hears people rushing toward him, grabbing the thing in his arms. He doesn't want to let go--*it's his, he saved it!*--but they pry the bundle from him.

"She's alive," the father shouts, "my little girl's alive."

So it's Xavier the Savior in a knockout, sixth round. The undefeated champ. You want something done, you know who to call.

* * * * *

Here's the kicker. The ambulance guys hauled ass out of there with the girl and her parents. Firemen came rushing up and pushed Xavier out of the way to shoot their piddly little streams of water at the house. Man, he could piss harder than that.

He turned to go, but a cop took him by the arm. Xavier resisted the natural instinct to fling the unwanted hand off him. The cop said, "You're a hero" and "Fate sure works in mystery ways putting *you* in front of that burning house."

Xavier didn't have a clue how Fate worked. He

didn't know what to say. He wasn't in the habit of hearing good things about himself. Especially from cops. What was going on here--police being nice, people patting him on the back? A photographer knelt down a few yards away to take his picture. Out of habit Xavier pulled his shirt over his face. After all, he had a reputation to keep up, and this kind of attention wouldn't help.

Another hand tugged at his arm. Xavier turned to see a man with a pad.

"I'm from The Ashfield Crier, Mr. DeSault--"

Mr. DeSault? That was his father. Xavier was just Xavier. Everybody knew him by that. The one and only. Crazy Carl, the oldest drunk in Ashfield, told him there had never been another Xavier in this town. That was weird.

"--can you tell me what brought you to this neighborhood tonight?"

Xavier stared at the reporter. Could he know something? Xavier didn't think so. He seemed like the kind of smart guy who wouldn't know a thing.

"I was taking a walk."

The reporter twisted around and pointed at the Olds a couple cars down the block. "The police said that's your car parked there." Xavier nodded. "So you drove over here to take a walk?"

Xavier going for a walk--he tried to imagine it. "Yeah," he said, "I guess that's what I did."

"How did you come to park so near the burning house?"

"Well…" He couldn't think, which didn't surprise him. Thinking fast on his feet was never his strong suit. The truth wouldn't sound good--*I was visiting my supplier down the street.* He couldn't mention Q. at all because he had a thing about flying low, under the radar, and expected his buyers to respect that. Having his name in the newspaper wasn't flying low.

"You live on the East Side, don't you, Mr. DeSault?"

He nodded.

"It's quite a coincidence, you taking a walk over here at the exact time a fire starts."

"Lucky thing, huh?" Xavier said.

After a few minutes he wandered away from the scene of the--what was it when something terrible *almost* happened? There had to be a word for it. He walked up the street to his cream-colored Olds Cutlass '78, his right hand burning like hell. He had to yell something and "Shit!" came screaming from him, even though he wished for something better. He was always yelling "Shit!" This pain felt different. He wondered what smarter people yelled when their skin was frying off.

He kicked the driver's side door. That felt good, and one more dent didn't matter. The sorry fact was he owned the oldest car still running in Ashfield.

It was an old Olds, a thought that would be pretty depressing if he were the kind of guy that cared about those things. He slid into the vinyl front seat that was so broad he could lie down in it, which came in handy when he had no other place to crash. He left the door open and the light on so he could inspect his hand. He remembered learning that skin was actually three layers of...well, skin, and if that was true, then he figured he had burned through about two and a half layers because he could see bare muscle underneath. His palm felt like lava was running over it or a thousand bees were stinging it, whichever hurt worse. He rolled down the window and shoved his hand into the cool night air.

Should he go the emergency room? He figured yeah. He'd heard of guys in the war losing their whole arms if the wound got dirty, and there wasn't much chance of him keeping his hand clean. But he'd been to the ER lots of times. It always took hours, and when he left he felt like hitting one of the doctors for wasting his night. When he thought about it, the only thing guaranteed to make him feel better was a tall, cold Bud at Ed's Bar. Eddie might even give him a free one, if he showed off his hand. It was worth a try.

Xavier twisted around to grab a rag from under the driver's side. He wrapped that tight around his hand and drove.

* * * * *

In big bold letters the headline said, "Man, 28, Saves Girl From Fire." Everybody would see it because in Ashfield everybody read The Crier.

That's what Xavier was afraid of--everyone reading how he'd run into a burning building to save a little girl. He didn't know what to do with this kind of attention. With anger or yelling or complaining he could just get mad or yell or complain back. But what was he supposed to do with praise, *praise* back? Not likely. He asked Cindy this in a very thoughtful way as they were sitting in his Olds under the bright lights of Dunkin' Donuts mowing through a bag of chocolate holes. She didn't answer his exact question, which he noticed was a habit of hers. She just licked her lips and said, "What's the matter, baby?"

He said, "All this is kind of getting to me."

"Don't worry, Xavy, you'll get into trouble soon and people will forget you ever were a hero."

Cindy liked playing with his head. She could even do that, laugh, and then say, "I'm playing with your head, you know," which was playing with his head even more by telling him. He was defenseless unless he resorted to physical force, which he threatened dozens of times by making a fist out of his right hand and massaging it with his left in a Jackie Gleason's "Honeymooners" sort of way. She said, "Touch me and you better make sure I'm dead because I'll call the cops so fast your head will spin off."

Xavier believed her. He already had been splashed with a hot cup of McDonald's Decaf and had to duck out of the way of a flying fork. Cindy was a dangerous girlfriend to have, but he loved her despite her violent streak, or maybe because of it. He wasn't sure which and it didn't matter because love was love either way.

* * * * *

A few days later he was shooting pool for buck a ball at the Curly Cue and told his buddy Tico that he wished he'd never entered that house, just kept on walking. What a waste--a gram gone, burned into his jeans. Who could he send the bill to? Answer him that.

Sure he was glad he saved the girl. She looked real cute when he saw her mug shot in the paper next to his. You wouldn't believe she was only six. Give her a dozen years or so and Xavier might be interested in paying her a visit, cash in his chips. Her parents said they would be eternally grateful, didn't they? What about a reward now, though, something he could put in his pocket? What was a little girl's life worth, any-way? He wasn't greedy. Enough to cover a few grams, that's all he was asking. Maybe an ounce. They'd be raking in the insurance money. Couldn't they spare a few thousand to buy him a new car, something at least made this century?

He hadn't visited Q. or smoked at all in the week since The Big Heat, as he thought of it. He had opportunity, too, and just said no, which wasn't like him. He couldn't ever remember turning down weed before. It went against his principles. But something happened in those few minutes when the fire burned the rubber off his Nikes and scorched his eyebrows. It was as if he had gone in that house as Xavier Terrence DeSault and come out as somebody else. The old Xavier would step over a body lying on the sidewalk without a second thought as to whether it was breathing or not. Not that he had anything against the drunken homeless, but there was a place for that sort of thing and it wasn't right under his foot. Crawl your way into an alley if you have to. It seemed to him that the new Xavier might stop, nudge the body with his shoe, maybe even poke it a few times to see if there was any life there. And if the guy needed serious help, what then? Down on his knees giving mouth-to-mouth to a ragged old guy? Was that where Xavier was heading?

He had been having dreams, too, and not the kind that woke him up raging hard. He was dreaming himself as a priest and a doctor and strangest of all, as a superhero flying around the city saving people from disasters. "It was like me, but not me, you know?"

"You're the X-Man," Tico said, "green tights and all that shit."

"No, man, I don't wear tights."

"All superheroes wear tights," Tico said, "think about it."

Xavier didn't want to think about it. The whole situation was getting under his skin, what he had left of it. He had always felt comfortable with the person he was born as, but now he wasn't sure what to make of himself. He had stopped at the scene of a fire and acted like he really cared a shit about somebody else. What was he supposed to do, keeping rescuing people? What did heroes do next?

Tico listened as he always did, one eye lining up his shot, but still nodding just enough to keep you talking. He sank the six ball and then chalked up his cue. He said, "Man, you can't win for losing."

Xavier admired the way Tico could put into words what you were feeling, even if you weren't sure what that was yourself.

* * * * *

He didn't like to admit it, but Cindy was right. It didn't take long before he got back to his old self, getting in trouble just like tripping off the curb.

It started out no problem. Ducking down the backstairs at Q's as usual, a couple grams in his jacket. He figured to head to The Pit at Franklin Square, find some suburban poser with cash busting out of his pockets, sell off two grams and keep the third for himself. He could see making a routine of it, every two weeks. Yeah, it took some effort to drive into the city, but he didn't like selling in Ashfield. Too many cops knew him.

He hopped into his Olds, rolled down the windows, lit up and drove. His mouth felt like he was chewing a big wad of laundry lint. Good shit, just like Bobby D. promised. He'd been going to Q. for more than a month now and couldn't complain once. That was a record for Xavier. Couldn't complain about the traffic, either. Cars seemed to be parting in front of him, getting out of his way. That's how he liked it. They were crawling along, he was flying.

He got to Franklin Square and couldn't find a place to park. That was the hassle of the city. He spotted a space on the corner, not really big enough for the Olds, but it was calling to him, *Park here and sell your weed!*

Can do. He swerved across two lanes and turned down Lynam St., then hit the brakes, a smooth move. He got honked at and yelled at but what the fuck? He backed in sweet. When he got out he saw that the Olds came within a foot of the corner. Somebody could clip him making the turn. But what the hell, one more scrape wouldn't make any difference. He locked up, feeling stupid doing that. He never locked in Ashfield. But this was a real city. You couldn't trust anybody. The car could be stripped in minutes. Or some dude could just pop the ignition and drive off for the fun of riding in a 1978 Cutlass. A classic. Almost an antique.

His tongue licked the roof of his mouth, searching for a drop of moisture. Nothing. He tried to swallow.

Couldn't. It was like he'd been sucking on a vacuum hose. He turned into the 7-11 and pulled a Vitamin Water from the cold case. Figured he'd wet his mouth and dilute the poison swimming in his veins at the same time. God he was healthy. Walking by The Garage, swigging the water, he saw some peeps he knew, asked if they wanted any trees. Buy a gram he'd match them rolling a fattie. They'd smoke, sure, they said, but no dough. Fucking useless.

Xavier trooped on. When he got to The Pit there were some corny-ass guys playing jazz-funk outside the metro entrance. Noise, that's what it was. A goddamn public nuisance. He was a rap man himself, wrote his own. Did the music, too, rolled a beat like you never heard anywhere else. He would have bust out right there rapping his head off freestyle but he wasn't at The Pit to put on a show. He had weed to unload.

Xavier saw a dude he knew—Carl, Kyle, something like that—the point was, he was always looking. So Xavier hit him up with the question. Wrong answer. Just another broke bitch. God, what was going on, nobody worked anymore? What was this country coming to? But Carl/Kyle did know a guy loaded with dough hanging around looking. He'd hook them up, a personal favor. So Xavier sat tight on the curving stone ledge observing the posers with mohawks and spikes and black leather. So last century. Few minutes later Carl-Kyle Whatever waved Xavier over to the side of the In Town News. An old guy was leaning there, cap flipped back, trying to look cool. Had to be at least 40. Goddamn ancient.

"What're you selling?" he asked straight out.

Xavier didn't like the question, didn't like the redneck accent, didn't like the fucking mole on the guy's cheek. But he had the weed burning in his pocket.

"Two grams, 30 bucks."

"How about 25?"

Christ, this loser wanted to negotiate?

"It's 30," Xavier said, then thought, show the guy some mercy. Reel him in. "But I'll match you first roll."

The dude pulled out the money.

"You fucking nuts? I ain't handing over shit in The Pit. There's cameras all over."

Xavier was about to walk away, forget the whole thing. But this guy had flashed actual money. There wasn't a lot of that in the Square today. So he went around the corner, down River Road, not even looking back. If the guy wanted the stuff he'd follow. He did, caught up behind Casa Mexico. Xavier sniffed the beans and felt like heading inside for a giant burrito that would last him the night.

"We cool now?" the dude said.

Xavier glanced up and down the narrow alley. No one. And the gate was open for a getaway. He pulled out the gram bag so the guy could inspect it. Just looked, didn't touch or even smell, which Xavier thought suspicious, or stupid. Probably stupid. Then the guy reached into the pocket for the cash and pulled out a little black wallet. Flipped it open with one hand, a cool move, and there was a shiny badge.

Just Xavier's luck. He wasn't causing trouble to a soul in the world and a cop set him up, trapped him, grabbed his wrist. No fucking way. Xavier balled up his fingers and before he could stop it his fist was heading right for the smug-ass cop face. Caught the nose right on.

Xavier and the cop looked at each other, both amazed at what had just gone down.

"See ya," Xavier said and bolted.

Oh shit. Oh shit. He'd just punched a cop! This was new fucking territory even for Xavier DeSault. He was running for his life, and it felt good. Some people ran toward stuff they wanted, Xavier ran away from what he didn't want. Seemed like you eventually ended up the same place either way.

He veered left down Lenox and came to one of the dorms, the preppies hanging outside looking over like they'd never seen a guy running before. He felt like knocking a few over on the way just for the shit of it. He was on a roll! He crossed the grass, hopped a railing and landed on the side of his ankle. It started to collapse under him, then snapped back in place and he kept going. Once a running back, always a running back. You never lose the moves. He swerved left and right, hopping rails, busting through bushes, barreling down alleys. He knew the secret to getting away from cops--run hard at the beginning to fucking demoralize them and zig zag to keep them guessing. Cops lost interest fast chasing a guy like that. A jackrabbit. But if they got lucky and caught you, it was payback big time.

After a couple of minutes he was fagged and pulled up. That surprised him, panting like an old sick dog, tongue hanging out. Time to get in shape. Hit the floor at night, a couple hundred pushups, a thousand crunches. In a few weeks he'd be back to his old self, Xavier the Man. The X-Man.

He took off his jacket and cap, letting his hair fall out to his shoulders. He stuffed his things into the trash container. He was sorry to see them go, but better to save your skin than your clothes. He walked up the street a little and sat down on the curb. Right out in the open in front of the Irish Eyes Tavern. Cops never expected you to hide where they could see you. Who would be crazy enough to do that?

Him, Xavier DeSault, crazy like a fox. That's how his Uncle Mel raised him. Taught him almost everything he knew worth knowing. He felt like a fucking guerrilla, the VC in Nam, invisible right there in front of you. His uncle said they melted into the villages, the jungle, the air. They could evaporate before your eyes. Shoot at them and they were like phantoms, the bullets passing right through. Catch one and you didn't even know you had. By the time the old guy was done telling stories, Xavier always felt fucking angry he missed it. A war like that wouldn't come again for a hundred years.

He heard voices, cops calling to each other, coming closer. He pulled out a Camel, tapped it on the box.

"Hey, you?"

Xavier looked up into the faces of two angry puffing cops. One of them was bleeding from the nose, the cornball face.

"You see a guy running by here wearing a blue jacket and baseball cap?"

"No sir," Xavier said, looking up and down the street, like trying to be helpful. He held up the Camel. "Got a light?"

"I thought he came this way," Bleeding Nose said.

Xavier put the unlit smoke between his lips. "I've been sitting here for 10 minutes waiting for my girl. She's late, like always. The bitch," he added, figured cops would appreciate that.

"If I ever catch that fucker," Bleeding Nose said, holding a handkerchief up to his face.

But you won't, Xavier thought. *You can't catch what you don't see.*

He waited for a few minutes after they left. Then

checked his watch. Cursed at being stood up by his girl. Even gave her a name--Colita, like a fancy Mexican drink. He liked putting on a performance. Never knew who was watching. He walked back past the trash container, considered fishing out his cap and jacket. But a blue and white might cruise past any second, have his description on their radios. No use chancing it. He rubbed his arms against the cold and went straight to his car. Seeing the orange ticket on his windshield made him laugh. He left it there, got in and rolled himself a quick joint. Sat back and blazed for a few minutes.

He thought about how big a hassle it was selling smoke these days. What kind of world was it where cops were the only ones with money? Made him think of Q. doing this every day. Of course, he didn't have to go out pushing on the street. Customers came to him, lining up on his back porch. Q. had it made.

Xavier started up the car and flicked on the wipers. The bright orange ticket dragged across the glass a few times, then flew away.

Life

There she was walking into the harsh light of the
courtroom--Gloria DeHaven, age 56, wife of Royal
DeHaven, who disappeared one day just as if the soft
earth around their house had swallowed him down;
mother of Paul, the accused and undoubtedly guilty
teenager. She sat in the first row and clutched her
brown knit handbag, which she had bought 10 years
ago because the silver clasp made a nice solid click
when she closed it. She wore sturdy shoes and a tan
pleated skirt that draped her rounded knees and
a cream-colored blouse with large cream-colored
buttons. Her right hand reached up and twisted the
breast button one way, then the other, as if testing it
would hold.

   She had worn the wrong clothes. The air in the
old courtroom was so stale and hot that her long-
sleeved blouse was already sticking to her arms. The
bench was as rigid as a church pew. How could she be
expected to last here all day? Her mouth felt dry, her
lips parched, her tongue shriveled. She couldn't have
spoken a single word. She opened her pocketbook
to find something to suck on and glanced over her

shoulder. They were strangers, all of them, watching her fumble inside her handbag for a cherry Life Saver. She pulled her hand out empty and snapped shut the pocketbook. A door opened to the right of the witness stand. Two uniformed men walked in, her son between them. She wasn't prepared for how odd he looked, a long, thin boy with such a bulky chest. The thick vest was for his own protection, of course, but what would the jurors think?

At least he was dressed well in a crisp white shirt and bright blue tie, much better than the last time she saw him on the TV news being led to the police car with his jacket pulled over his head. She hadn't needed to see his face--she recognized his White Zombie T-shirt. How many times had she washed and folded it, telling herself that it was just a shirt, resisting the temptation to rip it apart and throw it away? What failure of will had stopped her?

He seemed uneasy to her as he took his seat at the defense table. He never liked being the center of attention, so this would be hard on him. She tried not to make it worse by staring. It was difficult for him to look her in the eyes under the best of circumstances, but she wanted him to know that she was not turning away from him. She would show up every day and sit and listen and pray that everything would turn out all right.

* * * * *

The courtroom smelled of people. Gloria wasn't used
to being so close to so many for so long. She inclined
her face into the aisle, away from the enormous gentleman next to her, her nose seeking some small whiff
of untainted air. She opened her pocketbook, pulled
out her scented handkerchief and wiped it gently
above her mouth. A shiver of pleasure swept over her
as she inhaled Lily of the Valley.

The rear court door opened and the judge strode in
like an important actor on a small stage. He had fine
features and a shock of gray hair falling haphazardly
across his forehead. He seemed like someone she
might bump into at the garden center, a pleasant mid-
dle-aged man. Was that a good sign, or would a pleasant man be more easily shocked than a harsh one?

The judge hammered his gavel, and everyone sat
up a little straighter on the spectator benches. She
wished she could whisper in her son's ear to sit up,
too. The judge would not think well of a slumping
boy. The lawyers made motions, passed papers. They
objected to each other, bouncing up from their seats
like little pop-up toys. She had the urge to tell them
to sit still. After an hour or so the judge summoned
the jurors. Gloria held her breath and counted as they
filed in. Three men, nine women--and six of them
old enough to be mothers of boys Paul's age. She had
prayed for women, and here they were, more than she

could have hoped for.

The prosecutor rose to his feet and walked toward the jurors, smiling broadly, as if getting ready for a friendly chat. Surely this wasn't allowed. Surely the judge would instruct him to keep his distance. "Murder," the prosecutor said, "is a terrible crime to contemplate, especially when the perpetrator is 18 years old. I don't have to explain it. My only responsibility is to prove that the young man sitting at that table in this courtroom willfully bludgeoned Janet Louise Santoro...over a six-pack of beer." The prosecutor turned as he was speaking and jabbed his thick finger in the air. Gloria was disgusted at this display. She could barely look at the man, the swelling of his belly, his full, wet lips, the swagger, the strutting. He said, "I suggest we leave it to the Almighty to understand what influences steer a young person toward such a ruthless act. It is up to you, as jurors, merely to find that he did this thing with sound mind and clear intent."

Gloria looked up from her hands, which she had been marveling at God's miracle of opposable thumbs. Wherever you looked in this world, you could see miracles, if you just paid attention. She assumed from the rise and fall of the lawyer's voice that he was done and would now sit. Instead he flipped over a leaf of his large yellow notepad and said, "In the next hour I will outline the state's case for you, from the moment the baseball bat wielded by the defendant hit the skull of Janet Santoro to..."

Gloria closed her eyes. She needed to think of something else, but her thoughts these last six months invariably came back to this--*murder*. In earth's first family, the murder rate was 25 percent. How was one supposed to understand that except to grant that killing was part of God's Creation from the beginning? He could have exacted capital punishment on Cain for slaying his younger brother but instead banished him to the wilderness. He even put a mark on Cain, a blessing of sorts, that no man should harm him. What blessing might this judge and jury see fit to bestow on her own murderous Cain?

Jesus wept, the Bible says, the shortest verse. Of course he wept, with all the sadness he witnessed. But did he only weep? No place does the Bible say *Jesus laughed*. Was that telling us something? She remembered the suffocating days of Sunday school when the only release from the sanctimony of the teacher was a fit of giggles bubbling up in her more times than she cared to admit. The square-faced woman, looking straight at Gloria, said, "Woe unto you that laugh now! For ye shall mourn and weep." How could a little girl hearing that ever giggle again?

At 4:30, the prosecutor's statement concluded, and Gloria opened her eyes as the judge gaveled the session to a close. Two court officers approached the defense table. Her son stood up promptly, and she was glad to see that he did not make them wait.

* * * * *

She was not used to hotels. She pushed the key card into the slot and turned the knob. The door didn't open. Gloria repeated the sequence. The knob turned promisingly, but the door remained shut. How could she be so feeble? How could she not open a door?

"Try pulling the card out right away."

Gloria whirled at the voice and saw a little man in an oversized business suit. "Of course, thank you," she said and reinserted the card, then pulled it out straightaway. The door opened.

She peeked into the bathroom and was disoriented by the image of herself reflected endlessly in the mirrors surrounding the sink. What kind of person needed to see more than one of herself? And while going to the toilet? She ran cold water over her hands and splashed her face. She dried off in a Turkish towel so thick she could imagine sleeping on it.

The bedroom was decorated in pinks and blues, which made her think of her hydrangeas just blooming by the side porch at home. Over the bed hung a giant painting with a thick gold frame. A few sprigs of some plant or herb floated on the white canvas, as if growing out of nothing. Where was the dirt? Where were the hands that weeded and watered this living thing?

She pried off her shoes with the toe of either foot and pulled back the comforter to the bed. The floral sheet underneath was ruffled. She ran her fingers along the fold, tracing it up to a slight round indentation on the pillow. Had a weary maid, perhaps, reclined here for a moment after making the bed and fallen asleep? Gloria lay back into the faint shape left on the mattress and felt strangely comfortable. She dozed for a half hour, maybe more. When she awoke it was dark outside the window. She had to admit the city was beautiful at night, as if lit by hundreds of white torches. She wondered how Earth looked from space, with intense patches of light scattered in a sea of darkness. What would aliens think was going on here?

She needed air. She ran her fingers along the base of the glass pane but couldn't find a handle for lifting the window. When she turned around the room seemed smaller, as if it had squeezed in a few inches while she was looking away. Her son's cell would be much smaller than this, and how could he bear it, a boy who couldn't stand his bed sheets tucked in around his feet at night?

* * * * *

She returned to the massive concrete courthouse at 8:40 a.m. the next day, early enough to get a front row seat where Paul could easily see her, if he wished to. At the security station she smiled at the guard and opened her pocketbook even before he asked her to. He didn't look up, just pawed through her things with no regard for disturbing the order of them. She entered the empty elevator and hit the "Close" button. Then she heard voices and the shuffling of feet. A large hand reached around the door and held it open. In front of her suddenly were the Santoros, eight of them, all with the same dark faces and thick black hair that she had seen on television. In the middle was the tiny grandmother, being helped on by two strong sons.

In a moment the car rose upwards, then stopped abruptly at the third floor. The doors didn't open. One of the younger boys pushed 12, the floor of the courtroom. The elevator didn't move. Gloria wasn't accustomed to irony but recognized that this was it--the mother of the accused and the relatives of the victim trapped together in a space even smaller than a cell. What if some monumental malfunction stranded them there all day and they ended up gasping for the same last breaths of air? Would the Santoros strangle her in the name of saving oxygen?

Anthony Santoro, the husband, glanced at her, and she met his eyes with hers. She had prepared herself for just this kind of awkward encounter, which she rather thought might take place in the hallway outside the courtroom. "I want you to know," she said, "that I would gladly give my life if it would bring back Mrs.

Santoro."

The man stared at her with such hate in his eyes that Gloria felt sick to her stomach. She hated being hated like this. "I don't want *your* life," he said. "What I want to know is, would you gladly give your son's life to bring back my wife?"

The elevator lurched upwards, and Gloria felt her head floating away from her, like an untethered balloon. She would not lie to him. She could not say she would sacrifice her son, no matter what he had done.

"I didn't think so," Mr. Santoro said as the doors opened on floor number 12.

* * * * *

"All rise!" the bailiff cried out, and Gloria felt relieved as the judge ascended to his place in the courtroom. No one could mutter at her now or brush past her more closely than they needed to. They would have to leave her be. The jurors came in, and Gloria found herself smiling at a few of the older women, despite the instructions from her son's lawyer. He had advised her to look fragile and numb. At a particularly gruesome detail she was supposed to wipe her eyes and shake her head to show that no son of hers could have done this horrible thing. The boy must have been possessed, by drugs, perhaps, or uncontrollable anger. They would hold him accountable—that couldn't be avoided—but not with death.

The idea of making a show of her emotions

repelled Gloria. She had spent a lifetime concealing her griefs. No one had seen her cry at the stillbirth of her daughter or the excision of one breast. She hadn't broken down when the bank reclaimed her home. No one had heard her complain at being cast off by a husband and left to raise a belligerent boy alone. She did begrudge Roy one thing--vanishing without a note. The police naturally inquired if they had been getting along. Not for years, she had to admit, and what she meant was, not since he'd come to bed on their tenth anniversary night smelling of another woman. When their Jeep was found behind the mall, she knew they suspected her. Didn't Roy often rail at her peculiar ways as their neighbors sat out on their porches on hot summer evenings? Didn't he call her dried out, as lifeless as the desert? Wouldn't that make a woman angry? the police asked. Yes, she agreed, but what use was anger? They could not tell her.

Weeks later Roy called to say he was starting a new life out West somewhere. When she asked him to inform the police that he was alive and well, he just laughed at her predicament and said she was getting exactly what she deserved.

Did she deserve this, too? To be sitting alone in a faraway courtroom listening to how her runaway son committed murder? Two church women had offered to come along, but she knew their hearts weren't in it. And besides, she didn't want someone sitting next to her thinking, *Your Paul did that?*

Yes, he did that--swung a metal baseball bat at Janet Santoro, the cashier at Discount Liquors, when she refused to sell him beer. He was not a boy who liked hearing *no*. Then she ordered him out of her store--he hated being ordered, too. Gloria could imagine her son's rage. Hadn't he lifted a bat at her once? But she was sure he wouldn't hit her. In fact, she understood his momentary fury. What boy wanted to hear they were moving again, to an even smaller home? Still, when he dropped the bat and ran out the back door, hadn't she put it away in the basement? Was it her fault for not hiding it where he could never have gotten his hands on it?

* * * * *

She felt almost proud as her son took the witness stand even though he didn't have to. He sat tall in the chair, owning up to what he had done in a calm, clear voice. It had to be obvious that he regretted going back into the liquor store with the bat. And he plainly said he hadn't intended to hurt Mrs. Santoro--he had never hurt anything in his life, after all. He just wanted to scare her. But when she yelled, his rage took over and he couldn't remember exactly what he had done.

Gloria felt sure he was telling the truth. She wished she could tell of the time he punched through each of the little rectangular garage windows when she wouldn't let him go to school wearing a bicycle chain around his neck. Or how he threw himself against the wall of his room when she took away the knife she found hidden under his pillow. She had seen his anger, and she knew that sometimes it turned him into an unfamiliar boy.

* * * * *

At the break for lunch, Gloria found herself sitting in the basement cafe of the courthouse, answering questions from a reporter not much older than her Paul. She did not want to give an interview, especially to someone from the city paper, which had called his act "evil" the day the trial began. But the defense lawyer said that her son could use some good publicity right before deliberations, and stories like this always found their way to the jurors. They would know that this boy had a mother who still believed in him.

"More coffee?" the waitress asked.

Gloria nodded. "I'll take a little hot."

The reporter paged through his notebook. "Just a few more questions," he said. "I was wondering, how do you feel sitting in the courtroom hearing such terrible things about your son?"

Gloria lifted the mug of coffee slowly to her lips. She figured her stalling was obvious--certainly she was no good at deception. What could she say, that she hadn't really listened to the worst of the testimony? That would be misconstrued--the accused's mother couldn't even listen to what her son had done? The Santoros might consider her inattention an affront. The truth was, she didn't feel she needed to know any more than she already did. Killing was a terrible thing, with or without all of the description. What did they want from her--to hate her own son? She said, "One learns as a mother to bear up. Things never turn out as one would like with a child, do they?"

"I suppose not," the reporter said, and Gloria realized that he probably didn't have children of his own. He would surely learn. "I think what shocks people," he said, "is that your son seems so..."

"Normal?"

"Yes, normal. People don't understand how a boy from a nice home can do something so evil."

That word again--*evil*. How was she supposed to understand it any more than anyone else? Evil *was*--that's all she knew. If God had wanted to rid it from the world, surely He would have by now. "God accepts evil," she said, "so people must, too. Evil is part of life, part of God."

The reporter wrote furiously on his pad. "You're saying evil is part of God?"

"God is everything," she said. "Goodness, badness, stupidity, happiness, wonder...and evil."

She didn't expect him to understand. Even her friends found her religious views a little unsettling. She tried to explain that even as a little girl she had felt *of God,* and so it was easy for her to take His view of things. Evil and Good were both of God, like two children, one bad, one good. He would love them both equally.

* * * * *

At the start of the afternoon session, the prosecutor stood up and licked his lips until they were bright and wet. "Paul," he said, and Gloria hated hearing the given name of her son coming from this man's mouth, "you don't deny hitting Janet Santoro with a baseball bat?"

"No."

"And you didn't just swing at her once, did you?"

"No."

"Twice?"

"More than twice."

"Three times? Four times? Five times?"

"I don't know. I wasn't counting."

The prosecutor thumbed through his notes, and Gloria could tell he was just making a show of it. "The county coroner testified to nine points of blunt impact. Could you have hit your victim nine times?"

"I guess so."

"You guess?"

"I'm not sure. I didn't really know what I was doing, you know?"

"You mean you didn't know you had a baseball bat in your hands?"

"No, I knew that."

"Did you know you were swinging it?"

"Yes."

"Did you see the bat hit Janet Santoro?"

"Yes."

"Did you see her fall to the floor?"

"Yes."

"Did you stop hitting her then?"

"No."

"Why didn't you stop hitting her when you saw the damage a baseball bat can do to a human being?"

The boy didn't answer. The prosecutor crossed his arms and waited. The jurors waited. The courtroom seemed like it might explode from the silence. *Answer him, Paul*, she said to herself. But what words could explain striking a person nine times?

"I didn't know I was hitting *her*," he said softly.

The prosecutor cupped his hand at his ear. "You say you didn't know you were hitting Janet Santoro?"

"Yeah."

Yes, Gloria thought, say yes if that's what you mean.

"Well," the prosecutor said, "who did you think you were hitting?"

She watched her son's head rise up and his eyes look past the lawyer and settle on her for the first time during the trial. The heads of the jurors swiveled toward her. The prosecutor glanced over his shoulder, saw Gloria, and stepped between her and her son. "I asked you, who did you think you were hitting?"

She couldn't see her son's face anymore, but she could hear him. "Someone else," he said, "just...someone else."

* * * * *

On the short walk back to her hotel, she bought a pint container of corn chowder at the corner deli. She ate at the small desk in her room, facing a large square mirror. She almost didn't recognize herself. The swelling cheeks, the silver curls of hair, the small milky eyes. She remembered Paul coming out from his first day of kindergarten and pointing at her hair. "How come you're so old?" he demanded. "Mommies aren't supposed to be gray." And her eyes. When was it he told her, "I hate the way you look at me. I hate your eyes"? She could color her hair, but how could she change her eyes?

Gloria finished her soup and took out a piece of hotel stationery from the desk drawer. She didn't know what to write to him. That she was sorry? Of course she was sorry that she couldn't save him from his anger. She regretted so many things--that she had to give away his cat when they moved to city housing, that he had to leave his friends behind and go to a new school. She was sorry that she was so embarrassing that he refused to even ride in the car with her. She would have gladly changed herself, but to what?

Through it all she had loved him dearly, and she truly believed that was the most important thing a mother could do for her child. But he had never been comfortable with her affection. She knew that years ago in the way his body tensed as she hugged him before bed and wished him sweet dreams. He always squirmed out of her arms and slipped under the covers. She often wondered what it was about her that he could not bear--her thick arms, perhaps, or an unpleasant odor?

Gloria picked up the white pen with Excelsior Hotel printed on it and wrote about the old metal army men she found in the dirt when she dug the garden this year, and the coyote staring at her from the woods in the back of the yard, and the porch door that swelled so in the April rains that she couldn't pull it open. She mentioned the penny jar that was just about full now and the large black ants that had started their annual spring migration into the kitchen. She wrote slowly, and the words spun out on the paper in almost impossible thinness, as if laid there by a spider. Sometimes she thought her handwriting was the only delicate thing about her.

After almost filling the page, she reread the letter and wondered why she was telling him about metal army men and staring coyotes and sticky porch doors, things he would never see again. She tore up that paper and took out another. She thought for a minute.

Then in larger letters she wrote, "I know there were so many things that drove you to that terrible moment in the store. It wasn't you, Paul, I know it wasn't you who did this thing. The anger moved through you and did its worst, and I pray that it has left you now and you can be at peace. God still loves you, as I do. Mom."

She folded the page in threes and slid it into its tight envelope. She wrote "Paul" on the front and then tucked the letter quickly into her pocketbook before she had the chance to tear this one up, too.

* * * * *

She made sure to get to court before proceedings began the next day to call over her son's lawyer. "For Paul," she said, handing him the envelope. The lawyer turned away before she could say that it was just a silly note, nothing important at all.

For the first hour of the morning session Gloria sat angled on the court bench, her good ear turned toward the final arguments. She kept waiting for the lawyer to tell how Paul had cried for days after his grandfather's sudden death. And about the old cat her son chose at the animal shelter when he could have picked a kitten or a puppy. How many boys would do that? He had been such a good child, everybody said so, as good as any mother could expect.

She hated thinking of her son in the past tense, but it was hard to imagine anyone calling him good again. She knew the year of his change, the very hour, in fact-

-noon on Confirmation Day, a week after Roy's desertion. They were sitting in the front pew of church. The minister called out "Master Paul DeHaven," and the boy stood right up. "Please come forward with your mother...and your father." She remembered her son's face. His cheeks burned red. His teeth were grinding. He balled up his fists and pounded the back of the pew. As she reached to stop him he ran down the aisle and out of church forever.

She had told the lawyer these things, everything she thought might help, but now he was sitting down without mentioning any of it. How could they understand Paul if they didn't know what he had gone through? Didn't *before* matter?

* * * * *

Gloria waited in her hotel for the verdict. She sat on the bed for most of two days, dressed and ready to go to the courthouse whenever the call came. She prayed some and tried to think of better times. But she found that each good thought seemed to lead to something bad, and she wondered if all lives were like this. She remembered a perfect Christmas morning that Paul called his best ever ending with Roy fabricating a fight with her so he could stomp out of the house and find his pleasures elsewhere. She thought of the last trip to the lake, Roy and Paul jumping off the pier side by side, but then how much harder it was to explain to him why his father had abandoned them a week later. She remembered Paul's Little League days and the surprise of the parents in the stands at how far this slight boy could hit the ball. Roy always said his son had a beautiful swing. And what would the proud father say now?

* * * * *

The chairwoman of the jury said, "Guilty, murder in the second degree."

Guilty...murder...second degree. Was there any other mother on the planet who could feel such happiness at these words? The jurors had spared her son from death. Anything else he could survive, she was sure.

"All rise."

The judge hurried from the court, and the bailiffs took the arms of her son. He stood up, and she saw her note to him crumpled in his hand. It was all happening so quickly. In a moment he would be gone from the room, and what if he kept on refusing to see her? Was this her last glimpse of him?

"Paul?"

He turned his head at her voice and said something, but she couldn't hear what. She pressed closer to the rail. "Paul?"

He turned back again, and she still couldn't hear him but she read the shape of his mouth and the words were "Fuck you." The court officers jerked his arms, whipping her son's head around. She wanted to tell them not to hold it against him, that he was right--of course, fuck her! What had she done but bring emptiness and poverty into his life by driving his father away? What example had she given him but to be plain and dull? What had she ever taught him that he could use in this world? How could she have thought to raise a boy alone?

She moved out of the courtroom, and camera bulbs flashed in her face. Suddenly she wished for a jacket to throw over her head, too. She felt guilty, even if she didn't know of what exactly. Perhaps she had blocked out the terrible memory. How could she know what she didn't remember? When would they come for her? And what should she confess to?

A reporter from the TV news grabbed her sleeve. The eye of a camera stared at her. "Mrs. DeHaven, are you satisfied with the verdict?"

Gloria blinked into the hot, bright lights. "Life," she said, "my son gets life. What more could a mother ask for?"

Eyewitness

You remember saying to someone once that most of life takes place when you're not paying attention. You thought it was a clever remark, but *the other* in that conversation—you remember the place, your cousin's wedding, but not the man at all—simply nodded and said he needed another drink. No matter. You decided at that point in your life that you would start paying attention.

What do you see as you enter the Somerton Mall at 3:32pm on a Saturday afternoon in October? A woman pushing a blue baby carriage, blond-headed boy inside, with pink cheeks and big bright eyes. Has a placid expression, as if life is starting out pretty well for him. You notice him as she passes in front of you—cuts in front of you, really, as if a mother with her newborn naturally has the right away. Of course you're just assuming it's a boy, the blue carriage and all. Perhaps it's not even his mother--a nanny, an aunt or just some desperate woman who has kidnapped this beautiful child some weeks before. There are many possibilities. She isn't dressed well at all. Gray sweatpants and a thin, tight yellow T-shirt. Clothes for lounging around the house or weeding the garden. Hardly fit for a trip to even a modest mall like this. No sense of style. Will the boy grow up wondering how he could possibly have come from her. Or if he did?

Five seconds perhaps, 10 at the most--the woman pushing the baby carriage in front of you, your thinking how presumptuous she is as you peek in at the baby, as all adults do, noticing his glowing skin, then her contrasting drabness. The brain can process so much in a short time without your even asking it to. Assumptions will not be denied.

What do you see next? The security guard standing by the mannequin of a woman with her left hip jutting up, her left arm stretched out and left hand tilted back in a painful-looking way. You've never seen a real woman looking even remotely like this. She's wearing a bright red dress, clingy fabric. This may be what first drew your eyes, the shape of her vaguely sexual. Then there's the security guard, a large man in his forties with a bulging belly draping over his belt, a former football player, perhaps, one of those never quite good enough who bounces from the practice squad to the real team for a few years, then tears an ACL and is quickly cut. Now reduced to standing in the women's department of Macy's all day facing rows of beige and white lingerie. His eyes should be darting about, looking for the single abnormal thing that hints at something criminal about to occur, but he's staring downwards, as if at his knee, the part of his body that failed him. Or perhaps his head is just too tired to hold up, a second job keeping him from anything close to a full night's sleep. You look away from the security man, not wanting to offend him, and away from the mannequin, lest your interest in her seem prurient. It can be perilous to let your eyes remain too long in some places. If you want to know what a person is really like in the recesses of his soul, watch to see what he watches. Watch to see where his eyes linger. Watch to see when he averts his eyes. Eyes don't lie. Perhaps you're being watched yourself, giving your deepest self away with each glance held too long. Watched by whom? Some minimum-wage, first-job kind of guy sitting with his feet on the desk in an airless back room, scanning five or six screens at once, hoping to catch someone at something suspicious, or even make something up just to rouse Security into action, make his job important for a few minutes, a break from the monotony. In any case, one must be careful, not knowing who is observing.

A few steps farther, sliding your soft-soled shoes over the slick marble, making sure not to slip as you've been known to do, not the surest footed guy even on a flat surface, you stand in the middle of the atrium. There is an imposing aura to the place that makes you feel small—is this really what the architect intended?--as you crane your neck back to see the large round glass in the roof, letting in an opaque light, like a cloudy lens, a cataract. You think of the sun as God's torch and try to think if you made up that metaphor yourself or read it somewhere. Surely you read it somewhere. Everything in your head is traceable to someone else--or more accurately, to other people, thousands of them, their opinions and statements and questions all mixing in your brain until you open up your mouth and say something that has the appearance of being original when all you've done is rearrange the ideas and formed the words to express them. Maybe not even that, maybe you take whole phrases, whole thoughts and repeat them as your own. Who's going to question you? Who's going to know? You're not a writer putting anything on paper. It's all in words that scramble off your tongue and disappear into the air. Perhaps if someone were really paying attention to you, they would notice. But it is a fact of life that people are far more interested in their own thoughts and words than to be concerned with yours. You're probably not even worth watching by the watchman.

Something happens. You don't see it, but you hear the scream. Screams, to be precise. At least two voices and maybe three, but not more than three. You sang your way through college, four years of chorus that gave your brain a break from the endless reading and interpreting of obscure Icelandic sagas, Arthurian legends, and Medieval allegories—the stuff of an unfocused English major. Bach's Mass in B minor, Brahms' German Requiem, Stravinsky's Symphony of Psalms... Berlioz, Handel and Haydn. You've sung them all. You've been trained to distinguish voices. There were certainly no more than three people screaming. You would make a great witness to this point if it came to that.

What do you do? Turn to look, of course, as everyone in the atrium does. A scream demands attention. But there's no obvious commotion as one might expect, no rushing about at the far end, the Food Court. You catch the eye of a young man with the hint of a beard on his chin just inside Leather World. He's leaning out to see, an expensive jacket in his hands, one of those fake World War II bomber types. Might he take this opportunity to hurry out of the store with the jacket still in hand, unpaid for? Would you follow him? Would you report him? Probably not. He could have a gun. Even the police say don't chase someone.

The young man does nothing so bold as to steal a leather jacket. He just shrugs that he doesn't know what's going on either and doesn't really care, then turns back to try on the jacket and admire himself in the mirror. That relaxes you. If he isn't running toward the screams, why should you? He's a lot younger, after all. By rights it should be him rushing headlong into battle.

Maybe there isn't any battle at all. Could be a rat scurrying down the aisle. That would make women scream. Yes, it was definitely the high-pitched voices of women, all three. And yes, men might scream seeing a rat, too. Probably even you. If not some rodent, maybe it's a menacing dog off the leash—some inscrutable chow or boxer—but then why no barking? A terrorist attack? Not here, not in Somerton, not at this mall. The terrorists haven't wised up to realize the fear they could spread by striking at an out-of-the-way place like this, or any small town in the likes of Iowa, Nebraska, Mississippi. Do they really think people in such states care about New York and Boston and Washington?

So what's left—a robbery? This isn't a bank, after all, where the money is, with black-hooded gunmen shouting at people to lie on the floor and not look up or they'll get a bullet in their head. No one carries cash to the mall these days. All robbers would get here are credit cards, some phones and cheap jewelry. Not a big enough haul for the risk.

You listen, you wait, but there are no more screams, no stampede of people trying to flee the scene. There's no unusual noise at all now coming from the far end of the mall as you turn into The Kitchen Store and try to remember what exactly it was that you came here to buy.

A Man to Be Endured

I read the other day that a certain type of leech copulates in only one place, the rectum of a hippopotamus. That made me wonder, how many other rectums of creatures had this leech tried first? And what makes the hippopotamus ass so hospitable?

It must be nice to find one's niche in life. I'm still looking for mine. Apparently marriage isn't it, because I'm being divorced again. Sheila, my first wife, used to say that I deliberately flout social conventions and cited movie theaters, churches, doctors' offices, clothing stores and barber shops as evidence. When was the last time I'd stepped in any one of them? I had to think for a while. When was the last time I called someone on the phone just to talk? A few months, I supposed. *Years*, she said.

Jill, my "patience-of-a-saint second wife," as she often introduced herself, said I don't know when to keep my mouth shut. I admit, I take conversation too seriously. I tell people that hope is only fear of the present and faith a substitute for accepting what is. Jill says this kind of talk makes me a cynic. But if I were more clever with words I bet I could say the same things and people would think me insightful.

Nobody wants to hear my peculiar opinions, according to Jill, especially at social gatherings, which she is fond of hosting. She said I was quite possibly the only man on earth with an EQ of zero. When I didn't even know enough to take offense, she tossed a heavy book called "Emotional Intelligence" in my lap. "Read this," she told me, "and maybe you'll understand what's so wrong with yourself."

* * * * *

What's wrong with me, she determined five years into our marriage, is that I sit in judgment of a world in which I fail to take part. I admit it--I see, I think, I judge. How can anyone not? Politics, sports, schools, churches, families. I challenged her to name one system where good was winning out over bad. She was preparing a lobster dinner at the time for a party of six. She held a wiggling two-pounder over the open pot of boiling water on the stove. The steam rose and moistened her face. Jill stared at the unluckily tasty crustacean with a tightening around her eyes, annoyance that he was squirming in her hand. Then she slipped the thick blue rubber bands off his claws and dropped him in. Perhaps she thought she was giving him a fighting chance. She watched for a moment, then slid the top on. I heard scratching from inside the pot.

I said I would eat on the deck and began making

myself a sandwich of hummus, sharp cheese, and sprouts. I thought I was being considerate, letting the others enjoy ripping open their lobsters in peace. Jill pushed in and out through the dining room door with dishes, mumbling all the while about the spectacle I was making of myself. "I'm not the only one who wouldn't boil a creature alive," I said as I fumbled to open the back door with my hands full.

She dismissed my observation with a wave of her free hand. "You wear your opinions on your chest like little flashing badges," she said, "and that's always embarrassing to see in a man."

That night, after the guests had gone, she informed me we would have to separate. My sensitivity to the "feelings of food," as she put it, was not the sole cause of her decision. She cited as the fatal flaw my refusal to do anything useful with my degree in philosophy from Hampshire College. I couldn't imagine what she had in mind. She said I had no drive or ambition or goals in life, and I couldn't disagree. There's not much advancement possible for a part-time handyman. Still, the money's good. It amazes me what people will pay to have someone else do for them.

In the days after my *embarrassing performance at her lobster dinner party*, she explained how our separation would proceed. She said she would, of course, stay in the house because she always liked it more than me. As I was left wondering about her choice of grammar, she hit me with the second part of her reasoning: "No matter what you say, I'm not the one moving out." I didn't pack up right away, of course. I never do anything right away. After a few weeks sleeping at the edge of our queen-size bed, facing the wall, she told me I had to find a new place immediately. "Separated people can't live under the same roof," she said. "You should have learned that by now."

She offered to let me take enough money from our accounts to rent for a year, but the rest of our assets she intended to hold as compensation for putting up with me for all of those years. Besides, she pointed out, her work paid most of the bills. Later, when *separation* turned into *divorce,* she even turned Sam, our old cat, into a "negotiable," as her lawyer put it. She thought she was getting the better of me, claiming this thing and that. But how could she start a new life with all of her old life clinging about her knees? My first wife Sheila was smarter. She divided our money in half as I marveled at her reasonableness. She even refused child support on the grounds that it was sexist. She said she didn't need any assistance from me to raise our son.

I missed the deeper meaning of her statement. One afternoon when I returned from erecting a lamppost for a pair of doctors, I opened the front door and found our home stripped to the walls. There were bright patches of wallpaper where she had taken down pictures, and the indentations of wooden legs where chairs once sat on the living room rug. A note taped to the phone said, "I've taken Danny to San Francisco to live with my sister. We had to get away--he gets too confused listening to you. I'm sure you understand. S."

She knew I would agree that our son was better off living with her. I am as she said, irredeemably anti-social and frequently under-employed, a poor model for a boy. She even called my ideas seditious, a word she used for its weightiness if not accuracy. I admit telling him not to believe in anything organized, especially religion. I discouraged him from joining groups, such as the Scouts and the soccer team. I encouraged him to doubt everything except himself. I don't regret sharing my opinions with him. But it scares me to wonder how horrible a father he must think I am if his mother had to flee across the country to get away from me.

I thought I was a good father, certainly better than my own. I never yelled at our son when he didn't do things the way an adult would prefer. I never minimized his childish fears. I let him go to sleep with his light on when he said he needed to. I read to him at bedtime, kissed him on the forehead, wished him sweet dreams. One night he crawled under the covers and called out, "What am I?" When I couldn't guess, his hand appeared, holding "The Little Prince," opened to his favorite page. He said, "An elephant eaten by a snake." I was sure then he could survive whatever reality life threw at him.

Twice a year he sends me cards, at Christmas and Father's Day. He signs under the printed messages as if they are his heart's own sentiments. "Your Son, Daniel Shepard."

I don't blame him for the formality. How would he know that I always carry with me his picture at age six, dressed as a little prince for Halloween? I send him letters through Sheila's post office box, but I don't know if he gets them. He never answers my questions.

I could have flown out to visit him some time--I'm sure she would have allowed that. But then, how could I have left him again?

* * * * *

I should have noticed Jill's growing discontent with me. The signs were there. As she was preparing her 40th-birthday dinner, which she decided to host for herself to make sure it went perfectly, I calculated on a napkin that I had eaten 42,175 meals in my lifetime, never missing one except by choice. It amazed me to imagine a food-delivery system so reliable that it could run without failure for 42,175 continuous oper-ations over more than 38 years. Wouldn't life seem more precious if occasionally one had to worry where the next meal was coming from? Or was that just my first-world perspective romanticizing hunger?

"So go on a fast if you want to feel hungry," Jill said as she brushed her famous secret-sauce marinade on the thick cuts of Pacific salmon, "except not tonight."

I obediently put on the wrinkle-free Dockers she laid out on the bed for me, with a black silk shirt. I looked perfectly presentable, I thought, as I took my place opposite the head of the table, in direct line of sight to Jill. I smiled and nodded, nodded and smiled as I ate her wild salmon and walnut-endive salad, resisting the urge to comment on the chatter from the four couples around me. Dinners went well when I said nothing.

Afterwards we sipped coffee, and Jill proposed doing a revealing exercise she had read about in a magazine. Each person was to write down the worst problem in their lives. These problems would be spread out before us on the table, and we would each choose the one we would prefer to deal with. I tried to catch her eye to wave her off the idea, but she took the few curious nods from others as affirmation to proceed. She handed out identical black pens and pink Post-It notes, then restated the ground rules. "Be honest," she said. "This game requires honesty."

I thought for a while as the others quickly committed to paper their worst problem. it surprised me how easily it came to them. I rejected *Mother with dementia* and *Brother born deaf* as problems more affecting them than me. Finally I wrote, *"Father ran off when I was 10 and I've never seen him again."* I folded the paper once, then slipped it in my pocket.

Jill collected the answers and counted nine. "There's one missing," she said as she laid them out before us. She looked at me, a reasonable assumption.

"I prefer not to play," I said.

"You mean you refuse to play?"

"Okay, I refuse to play."

It was uncharacteristic of her to give up the argument so quickly, but she was eager to continue the revealing exercise. She read off the confessed calamities--lifelong back pain, diabetes, alcoholic father, a child with leukemia, insomnia, divorce, bankruptcy, alcoholic mother, childlessness--that one I assumed was Jill's. Then she passed out more pink Post-Its and asked everyone to write down which one of these ailments they would take for themselves, if they could choose. "Be honest," she instructed again. Eight people picked their own familiar afflictions, which was, of course, the point of the exercise. Jill chose divorce.

Before bed that night her anger propelled her through my whole character of faults. She called me incorrigible, inconsiderate, selfish, sarcastic and irresponsible. "Yes," I said, "so what's your point?" She threw a lamp at me. She said I would never change, and it surprised me that she had ever thought I would.

I always tried to balance her outbursts with great

equanimity, and she called my calmness perverse. The strategy never worked anyway. I soon reached the limit of quietness, which is silence. But there didn't seem to be any end to how much noise my wife could make.

* * * * *

She was repotting plants when she declared me unremittingly clueless. I admired the way she could so deftly move the gardenias, ivies and ficuses from smaller to larger pots without injuring the delicate roots. And she still had enough attention left over to catalogue the great faults of my personality. More seemed to occur to her day by day, like mounting circumstantial evidence. She came to scrutinize my every casual comment as if it bore deeper meaning, some intended insult.

"We're white wine drinkers," I said one evening out at a tiresome affair, a pre-wedding dinner. It seemed to me an innocent enough remark--descriptive, factual and totally insignificant. Will, the brother of the groom, a man neither my wife nor I had ever seen before, nodded as if he understood perfectly, retracted the bottle of red wine in his left hand and poured from the bottle of white in his right. He reached across me to fill Jill's glass, and it took him a few moments to realize that he was pouring into the fruit salad. He jerked back the bottle with a confused expression. Hadn't she held her glass out to him?

Hadn't he aimed right? He looked at Jill for answers. She was clutching her glass to her chest with one hand and with the other, dabbing at the drops of wine that had spilled on the linen table cloth. She seemed to be trying to rub them in rather than out.

Later, as we were heading down the rainy street to our car, she walked a step ahead of me, out from under my umbrella. "What's the matter?" I asked her as we climbed into our car.

"Nothing's the *matter*," she said, spitting the last word off her lips as if it were distasteful. "I just wish you wouldn't put a label on me. You know I hate that."

Her accusation surprised me. Of all people I knew, I was the one who most resisted labels. "When did I do that?"

She shook her head in brief disgust, as if my not knowing was more proof of insensitivity. "At dinner, when Will offered us wine." I remembered the spilling of the wine, but I couldn't imagine how I was responsible. "You told him that we only drink white wine," she said. "It may surprise you to know that sometimes I like red wine."

That did surprise me. At restaurants, she regularly ordered any Chardonnay, Sauvignon Blanc or Chablis on the menu, never a red or even a blush. "You do always drink white wine," I said.

"Not *always*," she insisted, "just *often*. I drink red wine, too--especially when I'm not with you."

"Okay," I said, "now I know that. But why does it make you so angry that I said we drink white wine?"

"That's not what you said. You announced to everyone, `We're white-wine drinkers.' It's like in that 'New Yorker' cartoon with the tanker going down the highway marked `Cheap White Wine.' That's what you made it sound like--we don't care what we're drinking as long as it's white."

"I see," I said, although I didn't, of course. On the drive home, she turned on the radio to some loud, fast jazz, music I had never heard her listen to before.

* * * * *

It wasn't just wine that I misunderstood about Jill. There were nuts.

She sent me for nuts an hour before guests were to arrive for one of her winter buffet dinners. She always found some last-minute necessity that required me to run to the market two blocks away, bundled up against the chill, head into the wind. When I arrived home, I poured the peanuts into a crystal bowl to be helpful, and she shuddered at the sight. "What's this?"

"Peanuts," I said, as if reminding her of a name she couldn't think of. "Planters peanuts."

"We can't serve Planters peanuts at a dinner party. You have to go back." She thrust the bowl into my stomach.

I picked out a peanut and popped it in my mouth. It was perfectly crunchy, and not too salty. "Why, exactly, can't we serve these peanuts at your party?"

"They're not right," she said as if the matter were settled. It wasn't. Returning to the store was more than I was willing to do to cater to her, even for pre-party peace.

"You asked for nuts, these are nuts," I said, holding the bowl. "I'm not going out again on a night like this just because you suddenly don't like peanuts."

Jill shook her head, as if I'd missed her point completely again which, I suppose, I'm in the habit of doing. "Cashews," she said, "pistachios, macada-mias--those are nuts that you serve to guests at a party. Peanuts you give to elephants or children."

"How would you know about children?"

It was an inflammatory thing to say, I admit, to someone who had twice undergone surgery to clear out her tubes and still couldn't conceive. I regretted the remark as soon as I heard it hanging out there between us. I don't know how I could have said it.

Jill's green eyes deepened, as if a great ocean had just washed over them. Her mouth relaxed into a bizarre little expression, like the archaic smile of those ancient Greek statues. My wife loved a good fight—both of my wives did, in fact. Jill flicked her head, and her newly dyed hair swayed from side to side. Her eyes fell upon her half-filled drink sitting on the kitchen counter. She grabbed it, and even before I could flinch, hurled the liquid into my face. White wine, of course.

* * * * *

The news of our breakup circled quickly in town. When I stopped in for my morning bagel at Annie's Bakery one particularly sunny Monday, Annie leaned over the counter and whispered, "I hear you're getting divorced."

"Actually," I clarified in my regular voice to show there was nothing to hide, "I'm *being* divorced. We go to court next week."

"Good terms, I hope?"

I shrugged that I didn't really know. "I'm leaving everything up to her," I said. "Her lawyer is drawing up the papers for me to sign."

Annie handed me my bag. "You mean you're accepting whatever she wants?"

I nodded. "She says I do that to annoy her."

"Your *not* arguing annoys her?"

It did sound odd, but I understood what Jill meant. When I trust her completely, it makes it uncomfortable for her to take advantage of me like her lawyer wants her to. She says I don't even know how to divorce right.

Annie shook her head in disbelief. "Your wife doesn't know when she has it good. I would have killed for a husband who let me draw up our divorce."

* * * * *

We bumped into each other outside the courtroom

shortly before 10 a.m. on a bleak morning in April. It was not an accident. Jill and I were always on time, one of the few traits we had in common. She said, "You're looking well."

I smiled and opened the door for her. "So, your lawyer going to clobber me in here today?"

She nodded, took my arm, and we walked down the aisle together. She whispered that the judge would be doing a service to me and all eligible women if he declared me unfit for marriage, from now to eternity. The words were harsh, but she delivered them with a little laugh. And besides, she was right. "You're not a man who should be married," she said.

"I don't know how to compromise," I observed. "I never meet in the middle."

"You don't even know where the middle is."

We stopped at the barrier rail. "We lasted almost seven years," I pointed out, "that's longer than a lot of people."

"*We* didn't last—*I* lasted."

It was a troubling thought--I had become a man to be endured.

* * * * *

The courtroom formalities took longer than I expected. The judge was clearly thrown off by my insistence on representing myself and took every opportunity to lecture me. "Mr. Shepard," he said, "since you persist in going your own way in these

proceedings, I cannot protect you against yourself.
I have read all the court papers, and I must say that
your world view is unique, to say the least. Personal
integrity," he pointed out, "is not holding every opinion as sacred, but distinguishing what is worth holding sacred from what isn't. Marriage is about giving
in sometimes, accommodating, compromising." Jill
looked over at me and nodded at the judge's sentiments. It occurred to me that he might be a personal
friend of hers reading from a script that she had prepared. Surely this wasn't standard judicial comment.

Then we were called to answer a few questions,
attesting to various statements of fact. When the judge
took a minute to scan some document in front of him,
Jill leaned across the gap between our respective
tables. "I wasn't really trying to take Sam from you,"
she said. "That was my lawyer's idea...a negotiating
tactic."

"You don't need tactics with me."

"I told him that," she said, "but he didn't believe
you wouldn't contest the terms. He said every husband does, even at the last minute."

"It's the last minute," I said, "and I'm not contest-
ing."

She looked in my eyes, then away. She could
never look at them long and stay angry with me. I
have vulnerable eyes, she said, and that's what first
attracted her to me. Soon she discovered my character

faults, and rather than shocking her, the social ineptitude I exhibited seemed to give her life new purpose. Clearly I needed to be saved from myself, and she was the woman to do it. Besides, she pointed out, there weren't many eligible men around who weren't gay, abusive or alcoholic. Apparently my main qualifications for being her husband were what I am not. For my part, I was attracted to the sheer force of her personality, drawn in like moth to flame, unable to resist even with the inevitable bad end staring right at me. It was her missionary zeal pitted against my utter intransigence, and we wore each other out to a draw.

"You didn't have to agree to a divorce so easily," she whispered out of earshot of her lawyer. "You could have tried changing a few things about yourself."

"I'm not very good at changing," I said. "I love you--that will never change."

She glanced back at me, and I thought for a moment that she might fall into my arms and say she still loved me, too. We would walk hand and hand from the courtroom, laughing at the bewildered judge.

Her lawyer tapped her shoulder, and Jill sat back in her chair. The judge said, "By the power vested in me..."

* * * * *

When I ordered a marble-raisin bagel at the bakery on the way home, Annie told me to take a seat and she would bring it over. She came around the counter carrying the bagel and coffee for me, and a bottle of mineral water for herself.

"So, it's done?" she said.

"It was done a while ago--I think that's what Jill would say."

Annie slid in next to me in the booth, and I could feel the heat from the ovens radiating from her skin. It occurred to me that I had never seen her below the waist before, never sat next to her, never smelled the sweet mixture of perfume and flour. She saw that I needed cream and reached for it from a nearby table. She moved effortlessly, like a dancer in full control of her body. She was surprisingly trim, I noticed, unusual for someone working in a bakery. Annie, apparently, didn't eat the confections of her own making.

She poured the cream into my coffee just enough to lighten it, and I wondered how she knew the way I liked it. Then she raised her water bottle for a toast. "To your new life...may you find what you're looking for very soon."

I raised my cup to hers, and the dull sound of the china against plastic made us both laugh crazily.

Bedlam

It's another slow night in Ward 6. Joanna says the
CIA is transmitting instructions to her over CBS and
won't let anyone change the channel. Bill the Lawyer,
as he insists we call him, came unzipped from his
elbow to his wrist and was rushed to City Hospital to
be restitched. He vowed to sue his surgeon for shoddy
workmanship. Jack wouldn't take his Dilantin because
the stripes weren't lined up on the capsule. He said
I was trying to poison him, and what kind of nurse
wears Army boots, anyway? Heather tried to hang
herself again from the aluminum rod in her closet. If
she keeps gagging up her meals, she may soon be light
enough to do it.

Me, I'm feeling a little better, thanks for asking.
No panic to speak of, just a little uneasiness today in
the cosmetics aisle of the drugstore and perhaps some
dizziness seeing my reflection in the Tiffany's window
downtown--nothing unusual for a failed anorexic. I
immediately closed my eyes, let my jaw fall slack and
breathed deeply five times. The feeling passed just
as the Calming Breath Exercise brochure promised.
Later, on my back porch, I smoked a honey blunt

Howie left rolled for me. I don't think I even need to smoke anymore--I could just light the cigarette and let it burn next to me in an ashtray. The aroma sends my mind into other foggy worlds where no one expects you to see clearly, because how could you?

Coming to work tonight has lifted my spirits, as usual. If you can't feel good about yourself working in a mental hospital, then you've lost all comparative powers. And isn't that what happiness is all about-- feeling better off than the next person?

Howie says I shouldn't aim so high, that happiness may be a bit out of my range at this particular time in my particular life. He suggested I strive for hope- fulness, which he said is the state most people live in anyway.

He's probably right. I told him that and he said, "You know I am." It scares me that he can see so easily into my soul. When I told him that I'd put in for the overnight shift for the extra pay, he looked at me with that squinty gaze of his, kind of like Superman trying to see through walls. He nodded almost impercep- tibly. He didn't say, "So there's no use my moving in with you if you're not going to be home at night" because we both knew that's what I meant. Howie rarely wastes words, just as he rarely wastes move- ment. At that moment he got up from the sagging sofa in my living room, smiled a little bit in my direction and left.

Bedlam

The first time I saw M. it seemed to me a pleasant place to be crazy. Acres of lawns gently rising and falling like a friendly green ocean. Giant shade trees with their roots heaving from the ground, perfect for cooling yourself in the stinging heat of August. Graceful buildings with lazy porches and massive central chimneys. A century ago the brick and ivy hid people with syphilis and dementia. They needed rest and peace and stayed for months, sometimes years. I could have lived there, then. Today the wards are filled with schizophrenic teens and jumpy heroin addicts and the genetically violent. Everyone is healed in seven days, max. We call it the "HMO cure."

You drive in on a curvy road under an arch of sycamore limbs. Once inside the buildings, there are no more curves, nothing rounded or soft at the edges. It's all straight and narrow and gray. The fireplaces have been cemented closed, the doors reinforced, the windows fitted with more bars. Everything is kept out as much as in.

Sometimes you can go a week at M. seeing nothing but the everyday paranoids and phobics. The doomsayers are still dribbling in but have switched their obsession from specific days to some more flexible dateless Rapture. They're mostly harmless, if you can stand their proselytizing.

Then you get somebody like Sam Gould, a 300-pound manic, the classic shitty admission.

Just a few minutes after Domenic dropped off our nightly four-cheese pizza, we got the call to prepare for a man built like a gorilla. He came through the door with two policemen holding his arms, and two more trailing. His eyes were smoky. His head was thrown back. His hair fell long and tangled over his shoulders. Gould went surprisingly quietly into the isolation room while we processed the paperwork. He acted the model patient. But after the police left he cried out as if his feet had been set on fire. The four of us on duty rushed to the observation window. He lowered his head and rammed the door. It was guaranteed to withstand any mortal strength, but I doubted it had been tested against someone of Sam Gould's bulk and intensity. Lester ran to the nearest patient room, pushed old man Robinson out of his bed and dragged away the mattress. We flung it up to the door and leaned our collective 700 pounds against it. Every few seconds Mr. Gould hurled himself into the steel frame and rattled our bodies. The door held.

* * * * *

On a night like this I miss Howie. I don't think it's healthy being a solitary smoker, just as I don't want to drink alone. There's a certain desperation to getting high that feels better to share. He rolls the nicest blunts for me, no spliffs or cones, just thin and firm, the way I like them. He doesn't smoke himself, but just his being here would be enough.

Bedlam

We haven't talked since I changed shifts. He texted me that he realized I needed some space for a while. He said he didn't mind waiting. Howie's the only one who ever understood why I surround myself with certifiables. I like the fact that they're exactly as they act. No pretense or affectation, which you get everywhere else in the world. I'm talking primarily about the maniacs and psychotics, of course. They have Ward 6 to themselves, and I often sign up to work there. You haven't truly glimpsed the human mind at work until you've watched a manic. It's as if they're tuned into a very weird radio station only they can hear. Their delusions are so grand I can see why they believe them. I'd believe them, if I were them.

It's a locked unit, of course, no sharps or flames allowed. The design is strictly Monet--all vagueness and hazy light. Victor the orderly suggested to Dr. James "Harvard Med" Riley that the psychotics might relate to a Dali on the wall or perhaps some of Picasso's Cubist period. When the young doctor asked if he were an expert in therapeutic artwork, Victor got angry and grabbed him by the lapels of his lab coat and shook him. Shortly thereafter he got reassigned to the junkies.

I'd have quit on the spot. You don't meet a high class of people anywhere at M., but the druggie ward gets the absolute dregs. Guys piss on the floor instead of waiting for us to unlock the bathroom door. The women all seem to have multiple personalities and won't speak until you figure out who they are today. I can't stomach any of them.

I freely admit that compassion is not an emotion I come by naturally. Empathy is even more of a stretch for me. It's one thing to feel sorry for the misery someone else is going through and quite another to project yourself into the nightmare of their lives. I'm willing to give compassion a try now and then, but I draw the line at empathy.

So why did I become a nurse? There's a very logical reason. When I left the bookstore eight years ago for nursing school, I figured there would always be a job for a woman willing to wipe up the bodily fluids of others. I knew I could do that. After all, I did it free for years for my father after my mother left. At the time I was a single 32 year old "without prospects," as Dad used to say, and I decided I needed a profession to fall back on. It seemed to me that the sick would always be with us, whereas books might not be.

Now I'm a 40 year old without prospects, except for a man I love too much to let him love me.

* * * * *

It's quiet at midnight. Mr. Gould suggested a joint might calm him down, and I almost offered to go to my car to get one. But Dr. Riley brought out the Thorazine, and now Sam is sitting in the corner of his room dozing like some giant stuffed bear you see in the department stores at Christmas. He has a big smile on his face.

My paperwork is done and the meds administered. So there's time to listen to Classical Late Night on the radio. Ray del Vecchio is playing Mozart again, a piano concerto I've heard dozens of times. Or maybe I've never heard it--I can never be sure with Mozart.

Music is good for me, my shrink says. It clears my mind for "important" thinking. Tonight I wonder, Why did I maneuver Howie out of my life? He didn't ask much of me compared to most men. He didn't need me to be there for him, or acknowledge him, or cultivate his self-esteem--none of those cliche emotional dependencies. He never hugged me suddenly in the street or held my hands too tightly in the movies. He always settled for a few quick kisses goodnight.

Maybe it was the way he had been looking at me so often lately, with disappointed eyes. Disappointment from anyone else I can stand, no problem. Who are they to have expectations for me? But Howie...

* * * * *

I started on 10 mg of Prozac at the beginning of my summer vacation. At the end of a week I couldn't convince myself to get out of bed, so my doctor doubled the dosage. She insisted I commit to weekly analysis--no more of this crisis therapy. I resisted at first because I'm certainly not rationally challenged. I work *with* them--I'm not *of* them. I scrupulously follow

the three cardinal rules of mental health: I keep my
clothes on, probably way too much for my own good.
I don't scream in public. And I pay my bills on time. I
learned that one like all my lessons, by perverse example from my father. He used to bundle up his bills in
rubber bands and mark them by the month they came
in, as if ordering them in some way was a step toward
actually paying them.

He said I would never amount to anything. He
said I wasn't even pretty enough to marry well and
bail him out. I always believed what he whispered in
my ear. As a young girl I watched the shadow of him
climb the stairway, fill the doorway, slip over me on
the ceiling. "You won't feel anything," he said. On that
he was right.

My shrink is very perceptive. At first she said I
was suffering endogenous depression and free-float-
ing anxiety. But after a month, she knew I was hiding
something, though she still doesn't know whether I'm
hiding it just from her or from myself, too. She says,
"The truth will set you free." Sure it will, and laughing
will cure you of cancer. Doctors see that all the time,
don't they?

Besides, I don't want to be free, I want to be gone.
I told her that: I feel like disappearing. She said, What
do you think that would feel like? I said, I feel that it
would feel like I had no feelings anymore. She nodded as if that made sense and wrote something on

her large yellow pad. The narrow lines on the sheet always intimidate me. I can't imagine saying enough to fill them up. Are her other patients that much more interesting? Sometimes at the end of the hour I sneak a look to see how much she's written. There's never more than half a page.

Howie didn't push me. Our relationship progressed like a long Sunday opera, no notes skipped. He waited 10 months before suggesting he move in. I said yes at first. But how can you live with someone and not accept his hand falling on your thigh now and then or let him curl around you as you watch a movie on TV? How can you go to bed with one man and see another coming at you in your dreams? Howie said I'd do just fine if I stopped thinking about the past so much. He said that's why shrinks don't work--they make you think more about yourself when what you really need is to think less. He insists I'm as sane as the next person.

Pity the next person.

* * * * *

I have no pity left. I wonder what else of me I've lost along the way--humor certainly, patience, desire perhaps, but not memory. Why is memory the last to go?

Fortunately, August is a slow time for craziness, so there are a few empty beds now. People prefer to be outside in warm weather, and there aren't any inspirational holidays this month. Just before Easter you get the messiahs with persecution complexes, and Christmas brings out the Santa Clauses and Jesus freaks. In summer you get a few agoraphobics and the odd delusional following dental surgery, not a very interesting bunch. Some bring laptops with them to keep in touch with work. They pretend they're on vacation.

"Johnny" was readmitted last night. He's the grandson of an actress who appeared in a popular Western in the 1960s. You'd recognize her face if you saw her, but her name isn't well known. She was a character actress, particularly good at playing kind-hearted whores. Her grandson's an obsessive who can't stop touching things and then washing his hands. The schizophrenics and psychotics don't know they're sick. But an obsessive like Johnny has some normal part of himself sitting off in a chair watching the crazy part get up and touch the clock or phone or television and then go to the bathroom to wash his hands until someone makes him stop.

It's no comfort to me to know that a person can observe his own craziness.

* * * * *

My shrink tells me my job is rubbing off on me. "Craziness begets craziness," she said. She recommended a change of scenery, an exercise at taking control of a different environment. So on my day off last week I drove myself to the outer Cape, one of those towns without a public beach. I parked at the end of a pri-

vate driveway and walked onto the sand carrying my
shoes. I was bold. I pretended I belonged there. At
the edge of a dune, a woman with painted red toenails
lay back in a low beach chair, angled toward the sun.
She wore a red bikini. A large Thermos sat next to her
chair. She was reading a thick book propped on her
chest. Everybody walking by looked at her. I imagined
being a woman like that, reclining by a dune in a red
bikini with men passing by. What would I read?

The beach curled in and out of coves for miles, and
I decided to walk as far as I could. But after 10 minutes or so I came to a line drawn in the sand, perhaps
by a child dragging some toy behind her to the water.
It was a thick groove, and my mistake was to stop
and think about it. If I had just stepped over and kept
going, who knows how far I could have gone?

When I told my shrink this story, she said, Did you
consider rubbing out the line with your foot?

* * * * *

The morning I tried to get rid of myself, I called
Howie and got his answering message, "Go ahead,
talk." The beep came faster than I expected. As I tried
to remember why I was calling, the phone hung up
on me, sensing that no one was there, I guess. I was
impressed that it could be so prescient.

I could have called him again, but what would I
have said, that I look in the mirror sometimes and
wish to see someone else? That some days I can't even

bear the weight of my own skin? That I look out of my apartment window and feel like dissolving into the yellow city air?

He would have sought reasons, first causes. I can't bear to tell him what his touch reminds me of. Instead I told him the triggers--an impending elevator ride, a crowded party, turning a corner and seeing strangers walking toward me. He knows it's none of these things, really, at least nothing inherent in them except the possibility of possibilities--the brush of a sleeve, a look over the shoulder.

How could I tell him that I stopped in the middle of the square today and closed my eyes and screamed?

* * * * *

Howie said he had felt my pain. He didn't mean it in that unctuous way of "I feel your pain." He said he sensed something wrong with me as he was driving across town to get a haircut. He felt a pull on him, a psychic hand on his arm. He did a U-turn and came to my apartment. When I didn't answer his ring he climbed the fire escape to my bedroom window. He pushed in the screen and found me in my bathtub, half awake, the water pink. He felt much stronger than I had imagined as he carried me to bed. He bandaged me up as well as he could and called for an ambulance. While we waited he held my head against his chest and rocked me in his sweet-smelling arms. I wondered if smell was the last sense to go for everyone, or just me.

* * * * *

It's another slow night in Ward 6. Lilly has started
speaking in tongues again, which is okay with me
because she didn't make sense in English anyway.
Rob the Musician threw his shoulder out playing air
saxophone and insisted on going to the infirmary.
Sal faked choking on his milk and spit it on the floor.
Irene ran herself into the cinder block wall a few
times, and if she puts on any more weight she might
just bust through some day.

Me, no dark thoughts to report, just a little disori-
entation when I combed my hair this morning and
didn't recognize the woman in the mirror. I steadied
myself on the sink and closed my eyes. The nausea
disappeared in a few minutes. Later, I curled up in the
easy chair to watch the Lifetime channel with my new
cat Sadie, a gift from Howie. She's a wild calico, climbing the curtains, yowling at the shadows of birds in
the yard, then chasing her tail in circles on the floor.
Exhausted finally, she fell asleep on my shoulder.
Once in a while she reached out her paw and tapped
my cheek. I didn't feel happy exactly, but at least I
wasn't alone. Sometimes crazy just needs a little company.

Visiting Hour

Of all people on earth, Shirley Cain figured she might
be the only one who liked being put on hold. It gave
her time to think about herself, which she rarely did
otherwise. She would cradle the receiver between
her shoulder and cheek, freeing her hands to sew
some new rip on Zachary's jeans or shirts. There
was another benefit to being on hold: she could be
productive at the same time as thinking, which to be
truthful, often led her nowhere but back to where she
had started. Sewing required none of her attention.
She believed she could sew in her sleep, if someone
just put the needle in one hand and the material in
the other. She even liked the hum-along music they
played on phones. With most songs on the radio you
felt like covering your ears to keep them from seeping
into your brain. That never happened when she was
on hold. She could relax.

What she thought about was this: Was she the type
who changed the picture to fit the frame or changed
the frame to fit the picture? She wished there was a
third option--like taking a hatchet to the picture and
chopping it into little pieces. But her friend Valerie

insisted that destruction, no matter how good it felt at the time—and it *did* feel wonderful--was not a viable alternative long term. Shirley supposed that she was a "change-the-frame" type, because the picture was surely more valuable than the wood that encased it. Valerie laughed as if that was a joke. "We're not really talking about pictures here, you know that, right?" They had been talking about Carl, of course, specifically his capacity to turn anything good in Shirley's life into ashes, and she wasn't speaking figuratively. He--

"Go ahead, Shirley from Millville, you're on WPEN, Prison Radio."

She dropped her stitching and pressed the phone to her mouth. "This is Shirley. I just wanted to say... hello?"

"You're on the air. Go ahead with your message."

"Sorry. I'm a first-time caller and a little nervous. This is for Carl--"

"No last names, please."

"Okay, well, Carl, I got your letter, and I *am* going to try to get down to see you as soon as I can work out the transportation. Valerie said I can borrow her Chevy as long as she doesn't have to work, but she works every day, so that's something we have to figure out."

Valerie--Shirley pictured Carl pounding the wall when he heard her name. *The Babbling Bitch,* he called her. He said she was part of the problem.

"Valerie's helping me line up day-care for Zachary," Shirley said, "maybe three times a week. That would be a big help. Then I could do the early shift at the diner. They pay $6.50 an hour, but some of the girls make $40 or $50 with tips just on breakfast."

She wasn't used to talking very long about herself. She was more comfortable listening, nodding once in a while, and saying "Really?" It amazed her how long people could talk if you just coaxed them along with "Really?" a few times. Carl could go on for hours.

This wasn't conversation at all. It was like leaving a message on an answering machine and not being sure the other person would ever get it. What if he wasn't listening? What if he was playing basketball or watching a game on the television she had paid for? She tried to picture it--a TV with glass sides so that nothing could be hidden inside. If only people could be made transparent. That would be progress.

Somebody would probably give him her message. He said that if it weren't for him, there wouldn't be a Carl in the whole place. In his last letter he wrote, "Imagine, a prison without Carls. What are the odds of that?" The idea seemed to fascinate him.

"Shirley, you still have a minute and a half to go."

A minute and a half? What else could she broadcast to 412 inmates? He had warned her not to say anything too personal, nothing the other guys could use against him. What would that be? He didn't say exactly. He never said exactly. He always expected she would understand what she was not supposed to say or do.

"Anything else for Carl, Shirley?"

"I guess I just want to tell him that everything is going great, so he shouldn't worry."

Carl worry? The man who bought a T-shirt of Alfred E. Neuman with "What--Me Worry?" printed across the back? He had worn it to her last birthday party, a round-number occasion--30. They ate at the Chinese buffet at the Kowloon over in Hudson and then rushed back for the game. She couldn't remember which game. She thought it might have been football.

She would have said she missed him, except she figured that sounded too personal and could be used against him. Did inmates tease each other just like six year olds?

"Thank you, Shirley. Next up is Beth from Mansfield. Go ahead, you're on WPEN..."

* * * * *

Shirley liked to think of herself as a woman who could adjust to any situation, once she got started. But she hated getting started. The first steps were always the most treacherous. She hated first anythings, in fact--first dates, first kisses, first births, first phone calls, first visits. She had always thought life should come with a dress rehearsal, and if not that, at least some stage directions--*laugh nervously, hide shock, avert eyes, exit stage left.* Why did living have to be so much trial and error? She often wished to *exit stage,* left or right, it wouldn't matter to her as long as someone pointed the way.

There was no exit in a prison. Just brown walls and gray doors and humorless guards.

"Step in," one of them said, "and wait for the other side to open."

She entered a dim, all-metal corridor, and the door clanged shut behind her. She counted to 10, then 20, then grabbed the handle in front of her and felt a buzz in her hands. The door opened into the bright light of the prison yard. She blinked a few times, and there was Carl standing in front of her just as if he had appeared out of the ground.

"God, Shirl," he said, "I could pick you up and twirl you around."

She would have loved to feel his arms sweeping her into the air like he did at home. But her eyes fixed on the corner guard stations. She thought she saw the barrels of machine guns sticking out. "Are you allowed to?"

"What do you think--they're going to shoot me for hugging my wife?"

She tried to smile, and she wondered what expression her face was showing. She wished there were more mirrors in the world so she could see what others were seeing in her.

They walked across the yard to an empty picnic table and sat across from each other. Carl's hands lay face down, and it occurred to her that she had never seen them so idle, even for a few seconds. They were always holding something, like a cigarette or rubber squeeze ball. She looked closer--his fingernails were long and pointed. She thought they must be fake.

"Beauties, aren't they?" Carl said, wiggling his fingers in front of her. "They don't let you have sharps in here, so the guys have to bite down their nails. But you know I can't stand doing that."

She turned his hands over and rubbed her index finger across his right palm. She always liked the inside of his hands--the bulge at the base of his thumb, the deep lines cutting from one side to the other. Perhaps there were answers buried in his flesh somewhere, if she could just read the lines.

Carl shook his hand out of hers. "That kind of tickles."

"Tickles?" she repeated. The word sounded so strange to her, spoken inside a prison. She pictured some larger man, with arms the size of thighs, stroking Carl's neck. Would he say *that kind of tickles*?

"How's Zach?"

"Fine," Shirley said. "He sends kisses. I guess I could have brought him, but I didn't know."

222

"And Alex?"

Alex? Just ten seconds on Zachary, and now on to Alex?

"He's moping a bit. He hasn't really been eating too well since you left."

"I knew he'd take it hard. They should allow dogs in here, you know? I don't mean bringing your own. But why couldn't they let strays in the yard or dogs from the pound? It would be good for the dogs and inmates, don't you think?" She made some noise, an involuntary assent. "Maybe you could write to someone, Shirl, suggest it."

She imagined herself sitting at the kitchen table, Alex's big furry head resting on her lap, and composing a letter to the Commissioner of Corrections urging him to allow dogs in prison. He would think she was nuts, one more silly wife.

"So," Carl said, "you're doing okay."

His tone seemed more like a statement than a question, and all she could do was nod vaguely. He half-rose out of his seat and called out across the yard, "Hey Charley, nice day for a picnic, eh?"

Another man wearing prison gray waved as he strolled toward the side wall, arm in arm with a woman who appeared to be half his age.

"My cellie--a lifer," Carl said in a voice Shirley was sure everyone could hear. "He was robbing a bank, and his buddy shot a guard. Charley didn't even have a gun, but he's just as guilty, that's what the law says. Crazy, isn't it?"

Crazy, insane, unfathomably stupid--these words did leap to Shirley's mind.

"Now he's got this woman visiting him every week. She read about him in the paper and sends him letters and pictures. They've got a relationship going."

Shirley thought she must have missed something. "He's in here for life?"

"Yep. No chance of parole, either."

From a distance the woman looked quite pretty, with slim legs and narrow hips. She certainly didn't seem like someone who would need to seek compan- ionship in a prison.

"Get this," Carl said, "she wants to marry him and have his baby."

Shirley felt lost in this story, as if reading a book with a few crucial pages torn out. "How could she do that--have his baby, I mean?"

Carl winked at her. "They've got these sperm kits. The COs will smuggle them in for you for a few hun- dred bucks. Then, you know, you do it in the kit, and they'll mail it to your girl."

Shirley waited for the rest of the explanation. Surely there was more. Carl tapped his fingers on the table as if he were playing the same trilling notes on a piano over and over again. "Then what happens?" she asked.

"She takes the kit to the doctor and they do the test-tube thing."

Life conceived in a tube--the idea had always fascinated her. She remembered playing with her brother's chemistry set one day and mixing every substance together. She imagined something magical stirring in the clear glass cylinder, but all she could recall was a foul odor, like a stew full of rotten vegetables.

Carl jammed his fingers together and then bent back his hands until the knuckles popped. His fingernails sparkled in the sun. They looked like claws to her, able to rip flesh from bone.

"Hey, you know that professor, the one who killed his wife?" She shook her head. "Sure you do, it was in all the papers, the guy from Yale. He's in here, too, three down from me."

Ah, she thought, such a classy neighborhood. They could never have afforded living next to a professor before. And Yale, no less.

"He figured he'd get off because he's this Ivy League hotshot. I'm the one who should've gotten off."

How would he have done that? There were five witnesses. They all saw Carl kick the man while he was down. Had he managed to forget already? "The other players had to pull you off Mr. Gagnon," Shirley said quietly. "You almost killed him."

"No, see, that's the thing, the fucking paper screwed me with how they put it. I didn't *almost kill* him. He *almost died*--that's different. He's out there umping a softball game with a bum heart? Give me a break. That's fucking ridiculous."

Carl swiped the air in front of him, and his fingernails flashed before her again. They seemed grotesque, like the nails of that woman track star whose name she could never remember.

"Keep it real," he called over Shirley's head, and when she turned around, there was Charley walking toward the opposite wall with his lady friend. Carl jabbed her hand, and she felt the prick of his nails. "He's from Texas, Charley is, and he told me the damnedest thing. You know what they do to murderers in Texas?"

Of course she did. Everybody knew.

"After they zap them, they cut up the body for parts and ship them to medical schools."

Shirley shook her head. She wasn't even sure why.

"It's true. Charley says Texas is the only state that takes parts from people, like kidneys and brains. Not just the executed guys. From homeless people, too. That's what Charley says. Then they ship them all over the country. It's big business."

"Carl," she said, "could we talk about something else?"

"Oh yeah, sure. I was just telling you because I thought you'd find it interesting. You don't hear about this stuff on the outside. There's a lot that goes on you don't hear about."

"I'm sure there is, but--"

"That's okay, if you don't want to hear, you don't want to hear."

He twisted around, one side to the other, looking anywhere but at her.

"Carl, I--"

He faced her again with a sly grin on his face that she couldn't decipher. "So I was thinking, you know a couple of months ago we were talking about having another kid?"

As Shirley remembered, she had been talking about *not* having another child and instead going to work full-time when Zachary entered first grade.

"I was talking to Charley, and this test-tube thing really works. All you have to do is come up with $200 for the guards."

"That's all I'd have to do?" Shirley repeated with an involuntary laugh that she couldn't stop.

"Okay, maybe it's not *all* you have to do, but that's the start. Just think it over, don't decide now." Carl looked over at the big clock hanging over the doorway. "I only have ten minutes before they call us in for count, so we should figure when you're coming back." He reached for her hands when he said this. She pulled them away. "What?" he snapped.

It wasn't clear to her what. Could she bear to see those fingernails one more time? Was this a first visit or last? "I don't know right now."

"Yeah, I'll have to check my schedule, too," he said with a fake serious expression, "but I think I'm free next Sunday. Can you get a car again?"

"I said I don't know."

"Okay, when do you *think* you'll be back?"

He hated her uncertainty, but often that was all she had to offer him. It was her most plentiful quality. "I'm not sure."

He gave her a look that she had never seen before from him, almost desperation. "What do you mean? You *are* visiting again."

Again she couldn't tell--was this a question or a statement?

He grabbed her arm, and his nails dug into her wrist. She clenched her lips together so she wouldn't scream. "Promise me you'll come back," he said.

"You're hurting my arm, Carl."

"Promise me and I'll leave go."

She looked around the yard. Where were the guards? Where were the cameras? Why wasn't anyone paying attention?

"Promise me."

She was sure his nails would soon draw blood, then he'd have to let go. Of all things, blood couldn't be allowed in a prison.

"Jesus, Shirl, just say it, will you? Say you'll come back."

She closed her eyes and gritted her teeth against the bite of his nails into her flesh. She felt like a shivering rabbit in the grasp of a hungry predator. There was nothing she could do.

He let go.

She opened her eyes and saw little arcs pressed into her pale skin.

"I can't believe this," he said. "I make one mistake, and you don't stick by me."

"*One* mistake?"

Carl leaned over and spit in the dirt. "So now we're judging whole lives, is that it? You're on the throne looking down on all of us in prison like we're scum? Well I'll tell you something, I've met some of the nicest people in my life in here. They stand by you when you need them, and they're always straight with you. I'd have any one of them live next to me."

And now you do, she thought, the perfect neighbors.

"It doesn't matter," he said. "You already promised anyway--for better or worse, remember? You didn't want a fancy wedding. You said it was the words that counted."

Yes, for better or worse she had promised to stay with him. But what about for worse and worse and worse? Was a vow unending, no matter the circumstances? Who could she ask about that?

"So you are coming again, right?"

There was another failing of hers, not being able to say "no." "Yes" was so much easier. "Yes" never required an explanation or any thinking at all. "Yes" always satisfied people.

"Yes," she said.

Carl flicked her nose with his fingertip. "That's my girl. I knew I could count on you."

"Yes," Shirley repeated with a little smile, and she was amazed that he believed her.

The Surprise Hit of an Otherwise Lackluster Season

Good evening America, I'm Johnny Motion, and it's time for another 15 minutes of...

AMERICA'S FUNNIEST HOME DEATH EXPERIENCES!

It's our 26th show tonight, and you've made us the No. 1 Home Death Experience on this great planet. America, you just keep dying to be on our show.

(Cheers and Hoots)

Wendy, we sure have a lively group of voyeurs tonight, don't we?

We sure do, Johnny.

Well now, is that a new see-through rag I see through?

Certainly is. Made from the latest miracle material--MicaLite, soon to arrive at your neighborhood Spray-On Shop. There's no need to take off MicaLite before bed, my friends, it just washes down the drain during your mineral shower.

Well, I'd like to be there to see that, heh, heh....

I bet you would, Johnny. Isn't he a real chuckler?

(A Few Laughs, A Few Cheers)

Now Wendy, who's dying on us tonight?

Well, Johnny, we have a DVD--

A D-V-D? What century is this, anyway?

Your guess is as good as mine, Johnny. It's labeled "Birthday, Number 34."

All right, let's turn our Vivron Experiencer on Sean Faroe, in Moosehead, Maine, and see what this D-V-D is all about. Are you there, Sean?

Hello, can you Experience me?

We certainly can, Sean, that's the miracle of Cyber-Feel, isn't it? Let's see, I'm sensing wet flannel, burnt rubber, and dog food. Am I close?

Well, I guess you are, Mr. Motion.

Okay now, go ahead with your story.

It was my birthday, I was turning 34, and my... my...

Don't be nervous, Sean old sap, there's only 100 million peekers on you.

....my fellow people at work--can I say the name?

Why not? This is still America, isn't it?

It's the Have-A-Ball Amusement Company. We make party favors for parties.

Party favors--isn't that about as interesting as you can get on this happy-go-lucky planet of ours? So, I bet you outfitted your own birthday, kind of a busman's holiday, was it?

Uh, well, I wouldn't know about that. We don't have buses up here, `cause we're kind of out of the way.

Okay Sean, I understand perfectly, you're way out there, continue your story.

Well, they decided to take me to this restaurant on the water, it's called the Sea Sense, because the ocean's right outside. It's a pretty swizzling place.

Tell us, Sean, what makes for a swizzling eat-in up there in Moosehead--some of that gill netting hanging on the walls, maybe a buoy or two to buoy the old spirits?

None of that, actually there's nothing on the walls. The fancy thing about the Sea Sense is the prices.

All right, I'm sure we all feel the scene. Now time's vaporizing, Sean--let's get to the death. We'll spin here in our new CyberLounge, and you voice up the scene.

Okay, we had crawlers for dinner, that's why we're all wearing the bibs. They were two-pounders--you really haven't lived until you've eaten Maine crawlers.

I'm sure I haven't lived, Sean. Now, that's you at the head of the plank?

Yes.

And what's that wrapping the old sphere?

A paper crown, `cause Jean--she's my boss--she said I was King of the Day. That's her sucking the meat out of the tail. And there's Jack, her live-with, the claws hanging from his ears. He was really submerged--oh, I guess I shouldn't say that.

Too late, Sean. Now we know Jack likes to soak up

a few now and then.

We were all under water, not just him. Anyway, he picked up the shell cracker, and he was trying to get Jean's nose in it.

Oooh, I bet that'd hurt.

It really does. So the Servo came to clear away everything and Jack ordered another round of liquids. Then he started telling this used-up joke about a farmer holding a squealer up to an apple tree to feed it. Jean--you see her? She's throwing Nut-Os into the ozone and snagging them in her mouth. She was always making us laugh.

What a mouth!

Yeah, it's sort of huge. I seen her put her whole fist in it once.

Whoa, Sean, I'm getting ideas.

Jean was always eating salty stuff around the Have-A-Ball, like Wally Chips, Nut-Os, and those new Bacobars.

So she had some foul habits, that's what you're saying.

We didn't know they were foul at the time, Mr. Motion. Anyway, just as Jack was getting to the punch, she threw a handful of Nut-Os in the air and caught them in her mouth.

Quite a trick.

We were cheering for her and all. Then she started hacking a little...right there you can see it.

Wendy, let's roll that again for the blinkers in our audience.

Sure, Johnny, here we go.

There, friends--Jean's first hack. Tell us, Sean, what you're thinking.

Thinking now?

Then, Sean, then.

Oh, well, I wasn't thinking anything. I try not to, `cause people say I get into trouble when I think too much. Jean was hacking a little, so Jack slapped her on the back.

Looks like he's really swopping the juice out of her.

No, that's the thing, he was just seeming. He didn't think there was anything really out of orbit. Nobody did. Guess we should have.

Cogito, Sean, no need to blame yourself.

I don't.

Good for you, I mean, there's still such a thing as personal responsibility, at least the last time I checked.

She didn't seem to want any help, Johnny--oh, can I call you that?

I'd be blitzed if you didn't, Sean.

See, Johnny, she's waving us away. I think she was embarrassed to toss it up in front of us, especially in an eat-in like the Sea Sense.

A swizzling place, like you said.

Right. So there she is folding over.

Looks like she's fingered a wipe off the table.

Yeah, she turned stern to us and hacked into the wipe, then turned back and smiled like everything was...

Hold on, Sean, I've been keeping track on our Atomic Ticker--Jean's been O-less for two minutes, thirty-seven seconds. She's straying into danger-land here. And what's that coming your way--the birthday cake with 34 rockets?

Actually it's a birthday pie--coconut meringue with olive icing.

Well I've never heard of that duet, have you, Wendy?

That's one for The Guinness, Johnny.

Everybody started singing happy birthday to me.

Sans Jean, I presume.

Excuse me?

Can't breathe, can't sing--right Sean?

Right, she was still hacking. And see there--she looks into the viewer.

Such a symmetrical woman, isn't she folks?

(Polite Applause, A Few Sighs)

Oh-oh, Sean, I spy a basic law of physics about to be tampered with.

Jean turned all of a sudden and banged toward the ladies room. Squished right into my birthday pie.

That struck everyone as hilarious, eh Sean?

It was sort of tickling, except she didn't get up.

That's Jack kneeling over her, swabbing the coconut off her face. You can see right there, his eyes popping. He realized that she was--you know.

Heading for the dirt, Sean, that's the phrase.

It's a sad phrase, Johnny. She didn't deserve the dirt.

Couldn't leave her out in the air. Hold on. I'm sensing...salt water. You know the rules, Sean, turn off the water works.

I can't, `cause Jean was kind of special.

One in a million, Sean? Let's see...10 billion people--that means there's 10 thousand just like her.

You don't understand, there's nobody like Jean. She hired people at the Have-A-Ball that no one else wanted.

You mean she liked to dive into the low end of the gene pool and rescue a few of the bad swimmers?

You're not making fun of her, are you Mr. Motion?

Let me think for a blink--yes Sean, that's why we're here.

I didn't know that. I never seen your show before. I just wanted people to know about Jean `cause, you know, she's O-less because of my birthday.

Remember our name, Sean--America's FUNNIEST Home Death Experiences.

I didn't send you the Experience to make fun of her.

Well, we had fun anyway. We always do. Goodbye

to Sean Faroe in Moosehead, Maine.

* * * * *

You know, Ladies and Gentleman, most of the time on this show we peek in at the exact moment of dying--and that is gripping, don't get me wrong. But tonight was kind of special, wasn't it? When lovely Jean turned toward the viewer, her pipe stuffed with those wonderful Nut-Os, you got to see the pause before perishing. She knew it was coming. We knew it was coming. Only Sean and his merry birthday-makers couldn't see that it was the salty hand of death in her throat, not the Nut-Os.

Is there a lesson here, Death Watchers? I submit it's this: If you're going to choke, do it at a cheap eat-in where you don't mind tossing up in public.

(Groans, Cheers)

Now remember, folks, unlike other Home Death shows, what you see here is 100 percent All-Real All-American Death--no fakes, no foreigners. When they die on our show, you can be sure they stay dead!

Next week we'll start our second season with a visit to the Museum of Deathly Delights in none other than the carnage capital of the entire galaxy...

NEW MIAMI!!

That's right, you're in for a very special treat on an all-new episode of...

AMERICA'S FUNNIEST HOME DEATH EXPERIENCES!

That's all the death we have time for tonight, folks. This is Johnny Motion saying, If you or someone you love is heading for the dirt, turn on the Viewer!

Chapter One

It's night and the air is spinning all around me. I've never crawled this far before, over grass and stones out onto the hard, wet street. My knees are scraped and my hands hurt but that won't stop me. I flip myself over and sit up straight looking out into the darkness for whatever might be there waiting for me. It could be something I've never seen before.

There's noise, low and rumbling. I twist from side to side and make all the sounds I know—grunts and squeals and growls. Nothing answers. I lean forward and press my hands into the street and push myself up halfway before my legs give out. I try again and fail. I try again and stay upright for a few seconds, my hands grabbing the air, then fall back. The noise gets louder, tingling my arms, like it's coming from the street itself. Out of the blackness two circles of light appear, giant white eyes. I open my own eyes as wide as I can, not to miss a thing.

* * * * *

The driver of the car coming around the curve hunches over the steering wheel, squinting through the blurry windshield as he coasts to a stop. Up ahead something emerges into sight, separating itself from the surrounding night. The man, tall and heavy, a stranger in town, gets out of his car for a clearer look. It takes him a moment to understand what he sees--a baby sitting in the middle of the road bathed in the yellow beam of a nearby street light, as if posed for some strange portrait. To the right, a small house is lit up in an L-shape around the first floor. On the second floor a single window emits a faint glow. There are no other lights, no other houses. He walks along the white center line of the road, the rubber soles of his shoes squeaking at each step. The child looks up, tilting his head in curiosity. He's wearing white shorts and one white sock. His chest is bare. Thin strands of hair curl over his ears. His fists smack his legs and then reach up. The man bends over, fits his hands under the small arms and lifts the baby to his chest. "What's going on, little guy? What are you doing out here all by yourself?"

He jabbers some sounds, an attempt to respond. His skin feels moist in the man's arms. His cheek rubs against the man's neck. His lips suck at the man's ear. He holds the baby away in the air. "Hungry? Is that it?" The small body wrenches side to side with surprising strength. The man squeezes him tight and looks around, expecting someone to come running, but the street is still empty, still dark except for the lamplight and the single illumined house. He points the squirming child that way. "Did you come from there?" The boy kicks and squeals. "Let's get my car out of the way and then we'll find out where you belong, okay?"

There's the sound of a truck coming fast. It swerves to miss them and the child shrieks, an alarm sent out in all directions. The man pats him on his moist bare back and whispers in his ear. "It's all right. I've got you."

"Henry?" The voice floats through the warm night air. Henry--such an adult name. It couldn't be this baby, and yet he stops screaming immediately. "Henry!" The voice comes closer. A young woman seems to materialize from the darkness. She's wearing only a light dress that barely reaches to her knees. "Give him to me."

The aggressive tone surprises him. "Are you his mother?"

It's a simple question, but she takes time to answer. "None of your business." She puts out her hands. Henry puts out his hands, too, and the man feels an obligation to return the boy. She snatches him to her chest and starts to walk away.

"You should keep a closer eye on him." It seems the least he should say, a gentle reprimand. Then he adds the absurdly obvious. "It's dangerous for a baby to be out in the road alone."

She turns back, and in the brighter light from the lamp post he can see she is quite pretty and even younger than he first thought, maybe not even eighteen. A baby-sitter, perhaps.

"I was watching him. I was watching him just fine."

"Then how did he get out?" He knows he sounds accusative, which is exactly the tone he wants.

She shuffles the boy to her hip and jiggles him. "The screen door must have got open."

She has the manner of someone you know you can't believe. "It's lucky I saw him before something happened." She licks her bottom lip, what would be a seductive act in other circumstances. Then she bites hard on the tip of her tongue, and it makes him flinch to see it. "You really shouldn't let a baby get outside like this."

She withdraws her tongue, sliding it through her teeth, scraping it clean. "I didn't let him." She pauses, an instant's reflection. "You must have come in and took him."

He finds the suggestion comical, that he has been riding around looking for an open door through which he could enter to snatch a child. And for what purpose? What would he do with a baby? He's done with them. "You know that isn't true."

She looks about, her head swiveling in an exaggerated range. "I just went to the kitchen to warm his bottle and heard him screaming and came running."

"He screamed when the truck went by, the truck

that could have run him over."

"No, I saw you carrying him away. That's when he screamed."

He feels the conversation shift under him. He's on the defensive now. "I was just going to move my car off the road and then find out where he belonged."

She shakes her head, her hair flicking back and forth across her face, more certain of her story now. "You took him from the house. I heard the door bang and came running. You were about to get in your car and drive off."

She sounds so believable that he begins to wonder how convincing his own story would be--that he just happened to find a baby sitting in the road at dusk...

"You're new in town, Mr. Simmons?"

"Yes, I moved here a month ago after my divorce."

"Why did you just happen to turn onto Great Bear Lane the night of August 3rd?"

"I liked the sound of the name so I thought I'd see where it goes."

"About how far is it from the street to the house where Little Henry came from?"

"Maybe 20 yards, give or take."

"And what is between the house and the street?"

"A driveway and sidewalk—that's about it."

"So you're asking the court to believe that a half-clothed eight-month-old baby managed to open the screen door to his house and crawl 30 yards over a rough driveway and sidewalk out to the middle of the road… all by himself?"

"I guess, I mean—"

The girl's expression turns smug, as if she has the upper hand now, and what will she do with it? "If you think I was trying to take him, why aren't you running in the house and calling the police?"

The boy jabs at her chest, and she jiggles him again. "Maybe I will if you don't go away."

He's quite willing to go, in fact wishes he had never decided to take a ride that night to clear his head, never turned onto the out-of-the-way road with the alluring name. But then this sturdy little guy with the curly blond hair would have been sitting in the road when the truck came barreling around the curve. He didn't believe in fate, but there it was staring at him, the face of Henry. "All I wanted was to make sure the baby was safe."

"He's safe, so leave." She hoists the child over her shoulder and carries him off. Maybe it's the involuntary bouncing of his arm, but Henry seems to wave. The man waves back and continues to watch the young woman until she enters the house to make sure that is indeed where she came from. It seems like information he might need later. When the screen door bangs shut, the faint light on the second floor goes out.

Chapter One

* * * * *

She stops just inside the door, holds the baby out in front of her and shakes him a little harder than usual. "Don't you ever do that again, Henry. You almost got me in a shitload of trouble." She sets him down on the thick yellow carpet and nudges a plastic elephant toward him with her foot. A hand reaches from the shadows behind her, circling her waist, and she leans back into the waiting body.

"Who was it, Jo?" The voice breathes into her neck, turning it hot and wet.

"Some old guy."

"He watched you come in the house. I saw him from the window."

"So?"

"He might come back with the police."

"I made sure he won't." She's proud of herself, how fast she thought. She could almost believe her baby was snatched.

He shoves his hand up her shift, pushing it out. Henry laughs as if they're playing a game to amuse him. "We have to be more careful, find some place different."

She reaches behind her head to stroke his face. She loves the feel of his cheek against her hand, a little rough. "Your house?"

"No, I told you."

She turns inside his arms, pressing the full length

of herself against him. "I could come for tutoring on weekends when she works. You know I need help in English. You don't want me to fail, do you, Mr. Manicetti?"

His face gets stiff in a way that makes him look old to her, like a grumpy father. She already has one of those. "I won't fail you, but you can't come to my house. You need to get your own apartment before the kid starts talking."

They pull away and look down at Henry chewing on the elephant's trunk.

"He already is. He said da-da today, something like that."

"When he starts saying `The teacher is screwing Mommy' we're in trouble."

She bends over and lifts the boy over her head. He goes rigid, his hands straight out, a mini Superman. She moves him side to side, like an airplane trying to make its way into a strong wind. "You won't tell on us, will you, Henry?" His mouth falls open in a soundless laugh, the thrill of flying tickling his insides. "Will you?" She shakes him till his head nods up and back, not the answer she wants.

The teacher reaches up to steady her arms. "Careful, you don't want to break the baby."

"He falls so many times once more won't matter. He bounces right up." She sets Henry down on the floor and then bends over to rub his cheek, back and forth. His smooth skin feels strange against her fingers, so different than a man's. Then it comes to her, an inspiration. "We could make another one. It would be all ours together."

He laughs at the idea, maybe even at her. "That's the last thing you need, another kid."

She tugs on his belt. "Let's go back upstairs. I'll shut him in his room. He can't get out from there."

He pushes her hand away. "I have to go. Your father will be home soon."

She leans in for a kiss and wiggles her tongue between his lips, then pulls away. "Sure you have to leave, Mr. M.?"

He pushes her back a little. "You're wicked, you know that?"

"I do." She likes how that sounds, two short words.

He opens the screen door, takes a look up and down the street. "I'll try to get away next Monday. Don't skip class anymore or they'll start asking questions. There're just two weeks left in summer school. Then you won't have to worry about English ever again." He says this with a little laugh but she figures he's probably right.

She makes a face at him and he's gone. When she turns back from the doorway, little hands grab her ankles and she loses her balance and falls against the stairs, which makes her angry, which makes her want to hit him or something. But that would just start him wailing so loud the whole neighborhood would hear. Someone might call 911 on her again and that's exactly what she doesn't need, the police nosing around. She lifts her shift and rubs the sore spot on her leg. "See what you did, Henry? See?"

He covers his eyes with his hands so as not to see a thing.

Part Three

A novella in which...

A boy learns his name at age eleven.

Boy, West Virginia, 1933

The pale thin boy looked past his pa into the dark bedroom where Doc Gibbs was closing up his black medicine bag.

"She's gone" Doc said. "You understand?"

"Yessir" the boy said watching Doc twisting himself around trying to find the armholes in his overcoat.

"Gave up fighting" Doc said walking by the boy and his pa down the old wood steps where the nails was pulling out of the risers. "Can't blame her the way she was suffering" he said over his shoulder. "I'll send Roy to collect her."

"Needn't bother" Pa said following Doc down. "I take care of my own."

The boy heard them open the front door go out and there wasn't a sound left inside the house. He didn't know what to do next there was no one to tell him which hadn't happened in all his 11 years. He stepped quietly into the room full of shadows and caught his sock on something that made him jump. He cursed in his head said "Sorry Mama" `cause maybe she could hear what he was thinking how would he know? "Found that pin you was looking for" he said bending down picking up the long shiny thing from the floor and setting it on the table next to her. It was getting awful cold in there he picked up the iron poker and jabbed at the logs in the fireplace. He sat close to the fire squatting down and the top edge of his belt buckle burnt into his stomach. He liked the feel of it at first but then edged back and tucked in his shirt.

Downstairs underneath the bedroom the boy heard the front door open again and then plates and dishes cracking against the walls. Pa wouldn't wait long till he broke everything of hers he could get his hands on. They didn't see eye to eye on much of anything like religion. He said church never did no one no good except for the reverend standing at the front door with his hand out. Ma said Preacher Daniel was a fine holy man and the boy should go along with her find out what religious people was like. Pa said he could tell the boy all he needed to know about religious people like Jed Holsen who walked around all day cross other folks' land speaking nonsense and Ma said don't talk like that Jed's seen God. Pa shook his head saying then God ain't worth seeing.

Every Sunday 9 in the morning she headed off for service by herself even if weather was bearing down on the house like wild horses. You could set your clock by when she left except half the time it said 10 instead of 9 because Pa didn't believe in Saving Daylight or anything else. When she took to bed and didn't rise up even to go to church the boy knew she was in a bad way and kept the fire going in her room himself.

The crashing downstairs stopped the boy heard boots on the stairs. Pa came in the room with a black book in his hand opened it up cursed some then threw the book in the boy's lap. "Burn this to keep the fire going." The boy saw it wasn't just a book it was Ma's Bible. She was fond of rubbing her fingers over the leather cover when she was awful tired and falling asleep. She said she'd dream of angels. The boy knew his Ma would rather lie cold than burn the Holy Book but Pa said the Bible was just another pine log that should have been burned long ago. The boy stoked the fire to show it was going fine enough without the Bible but Pa said "Burn it." The boy threw the book in. Nothing happened. The Bible just lay there like some rock that wouldn't catch it was a miracle. Pa stomped on the floor the logs shifted a little and the Bible suddenly roared up. The boy fell backwards away from the heat and Pa laughed patted his thigh and left. The boy looked back over his shoulder at his mama. Her eyes were tight shut and the boy thought it good she couldn't see the way Pa was carrying on now she wouldn't ever have to see Pa carrying on again and the boy said Ma you're better off wherever you are than here.

* * * * *

Morning broke over the boy in a wave of light. He

opened his eyes covered them with his arm and tried to figure what he was waking up to. Ma was dead. He tried thinking different ways about it but it still came out to the same thing. She was lying in the bed down the hall she was never getting up from that bed she was gone. He knew that the night before but now it was daylight and he knew it in a different way. He felt the sadness of it drip out of his eyes. After a while the boy raised his head up his pillow was soaked. He had to keep his wits about him otherwise the world would take more from him than give like Ma always said. He was shivering cold but he was even more hungry than cold so he went downstairs. There was no sign of Pa except the mess of plates and pots and tables and chairs thrown about the room like a tornado had come through lifted everything up tossed it around and dropped it again. The boy stepped over the pieces found one thing left standing it was the piano bench. He lowered himself down easy to make sure the bench held him. The row of ivories sagged bad in the middle where most of the good notes was. Still Ma played her hymns night after night sometimes she sang and he'd sit in Grandpa's big chair listening. One key far down on the left the boy touched with his pointing finger. The key felt smooth and slippery and the sound it made was low like the final note of the world being played right there in his house.

Grandpa's old clock started gonging from somewhere under the mess. It gonged two short times which meant it was quarter past something. The boy got down on his knees and pushed away boxes and bags of Lord knows what he pushed away broken plates and torn-up clothes till he saw the face of the clock. It said quarter past 9. Laying there on the floor on his belly he smelled something next to him it was whiskey it was Pa.

A hand reached out from under a pile of old clothes grabbed the boy. "She dead?"

Pa had seen everything he had so why was he asking?

"She dead boy?" Pa yelled at him. "She deader than anything you ever seen?"

"She's deader Pa."

"Good" he said letting go the boy's sleeve sinking back to the floor. "It would be just like her pretending to give a man false hope."

The boy thought about how his Ma looked. "I don't think she could be pretending that good."

Pa laid his head back on a pile of clothes and started breathing heavy and slow.

The boy got up to look for food. Under the sink near the rat poison was the crackers he'd seen Pa hide away. But the boy didn't have much appetite for anything under there since he found the old black thing sick and squirmy. He scraped the cupboard for buckwheat mix found enough for half a cake it wasn't worth trying to light the stove for that. There was milk to fill half a cup and an apple lying by the basement door with a bite out of it. The boy wished he hadn't woke up so soon. Sleeping was the only thing you could do in the world and not feel hungry. The boy dropped down on the floor beside his Pa and got as close as he dared. At least he was warm and breathing.

* * * * *

The boy woke again he felt cold coming on him he looked over the front door was open some. Pa never bothered to shut it tight Ma said they might as well live in a barn. The boy got up walked to the kitchen sink splashed some water on his face. He looked in the mirror Pa put there to shave himself. The boy stared at himself he never noticed before the way his nose tilted off to one side and with the long eyelashes and the thin cheeks he looked just like his ma. He smiled at the face in the mirror it was just like smiling at her. After he was done fixing himself as good as could be he figured he'd go outside to see what the world was up to. He went upstairs to get his boots and looked in her room she was laid out on the bed stiff as Pa's undershorts hanging on the clothesline all winter. "I'll be going out" he called to her. He started past the door but then stopped himself it weren't right for a boy to neglect his ma the dead have needs too. He took a deep breath walked in the room talking to her about how the day looked outside. The blankets was lying cockeyed on top of her and he climbed on the bed to fix them. He straightened out the sheet first pulled it up to her chin tucked it in around her how she liked. Then he pulled up the quilt and the lap blanket she used to keep on her knees when she was sewing and listening to the radio. He thought he was done but when he twisted around he saw the afghan in a pile on the floor. He grabbed for it spread the black and red patches over the bed.

Now he was done what he'd come in for he could leave but he didn't. He looked at her. She didn't look too good even for being dead. Her cheeks were tight like a plastic bag had been stretched over them. Her lips were purple. She looked about half of herself like the stuffing was pulled out. The boy guessed that was the soul taking off wherever it went there was no reason for the soul to hang around this house that was for sure. He started feeling sickness in his stomach he didn't know if it was not eating enough or smelling too much. He understood now the reason people put bodies under the ground as fast as they did. But still no matter how she smelled the boy liked having his ma there in bed where she'd been for so long it just seemed right. He leaned up over her to give her a kiss on her forehead like he did every morning he heard a heavy footstep coming up the stairs. He twisted round at the sound his hand slid out from under him and he fell on his ma.

"What in the Lord Almighty's going on there?"

It wasn't Pa it was the Sheriff. The boy rolled off the bed and jumped up. "Nothing."

The Sheriff stepped closer. "That's your dead Ma there boy."

"I know who it is."

"Don't be back-talking to me I saw you lying on top of her of all the skunking things to do this beats all she's your ma." The Sheriff stepped closer the boy stepped back. "I should shake the brains out of you" Sheriff said "but it would be a waste of good effort." He swung out his long arm cuffed the boy on the ear.

"I ain't done nothing."

"Then you were going to if I hadn't stepped in. Where's your pa?"

The boy shrugged.

"Figures. If there's something to be taken care of your pa's nowhere to be found. You bust up things downstairs?"

"No sir."

"Then I suppose it was that good-for-nothing. You come down with me and stay out of this room till your ma's taken. You understand?" He swatted the boy's head again.

The boy nodded and rubbed his ear.

"I'm going to town I'll tell you I have more to do than come all the way out here trying to sort this kind of thing. Your ma's dead she needs burying I'll be telling Roy to come get her no matter what your pa says. Now you stay out of trouble leave your poor dead ma alone."

* * * * *

Snow started falling past the window the boy pressed his nose to it watching Sheriff leave. It wasn't supposed to snow in these parts in April Pa said but that's what it was doing anyways. The boy felt awful cold without the fire going downstairs and no more wood on the porch dry enough to burn. He could run out in the snow see if there was any wood left in the shed but that would just make him colder. He was awful hungry too. He looked around the kitchen trying to find something he missed for breakfast. And there before his eyes was a bag of peanuts sitting on the stove just like it sprang from nothing. He ripped open the package poured the peanuts in his mouth leaving two so Pa couldn't say he finished them. Then the boy couldn't resist his hand lifted the package to his mouth again shook it and the last two peanuts dropped on his tongue.

He was thirsty now he ran some water into the scoop of his hand and sucked it down. The boy poked around the kitchen some more looking everywhere all he found was a crust of bread that fell off the refrigerator got stuck next to the wall. It was so hard he soaked it in a bowl of water for a minute then drank it down a new way of eating bread. Even with the peanuts and the bread his insides still felt sore as if they were eating themselves and not much liking the taste. He could see that the worst thing about going hungry was having nothing to do except think about it. If only Rebel was still alive he could take her out jumping in the air with her catching snowflakes. That dog turned out all right she followed him around and sat when he told her to at least if she felt like it. Every night she scratched and pawed at the door till she was let out to hunt in the dark came back in the morning with all sorts of strange animals that was hard to recognize in all the blood. Rebel died the second winter meeting something bigger in the night came home limping and bleeding. The boy figured she just wanted to die with somebody holding her. He cried for days missing Rebel funny how he hadn't cried yet for his ma.

The boy went up to his room since Sheriff said stay put and laid back on his bed. No sooner he drifted off the blankets were pulled from him he opened his eyes trying to make sense of it there was Pa fuming at him. "What did you tell Sheriff Wills?"

"Nothing Pa."

"Tell him I'm no good did you?"

"No sir."

"Tell him I ran out on you?"

"No sir."

"Don't lie" Pa raised his hand. "Sheriff came meddling down at Jake's said my boy was doing things I taught him. You's old enough to be let alone boy" Pa shouted.

"Yes sir."

"They ain't taking you away I'm telling you we's family and you don't trust nobody else you understand me?"

"Yes Pa."

"That Sheriff comes around here again threatening my boy I'll sue him that's what I'll do. He ain't got no right. If there's any threatening being done in this house I'll do it." Pa laughed a little at that but the boy didn't see the humor of the situation. "How old you now?

"Little more than 11."

"You tasted whiskey?"

The boy shook his head.

"Eleven years old and you never tasted nothing stronger than cow's piss? We gonna change that right now."

He led the boy downstairs to the cabinet under the kitchen counter bringing out half a bottle of whiskey. He drank a mouthful himself it dripped out his lips and down the roughness of his chin then he held it out for the boy.

"I'm more hungry than thirsty Pa."

Pa pushed the bottle in the boy's stomach. "You take what's given you. You don't say nothing when somebody offers you something except to ask for more."

The boy held the bottle between two hands tipping it up slowly to get just a taste then Pa's hand quick shoved the whiskey up and the stinging liquid poured into the boy. He gulped three times and coughed and finally breathed again. His stomach was firing like a coal furnace. He straightened up rubbing under his sweater where everything was flaming.

Pa laughed. "I guess you ain't a man yet."

"Close enough" the boy said stretching tall as he could.

* * * * *

Next morning he woke stood up but the room wouldn't stay still he had to hold onto the bed posts to get himself to the door. His insides were feeling all shook up like nothing was in the right place. Whenever he felt bad like this Mama always had something to give him from the cabinet in the bathroom or she fixed him up in Grandpa's big chair and fed him soup and crackers till his insides calmed down. He went downstairs found Pa sitting at the kitchen table where he had left him the night before. The boy sat backwards on a chair resting his chin on the back of it waiting for his pa to wake himself. After fifteen minutes he stirred one eye open then it dropped shut again. Another half hour he reared back all of a sudden wiping his eyes.

The boy said "I'm feeling kind of sick."

Pa stood up his legs wobbling under him. "Get me to the door" he said and the boy rushed around the table. He walked him to the door and pulled it open. Pa opened his fly and leaning against the boy leaked yellow on the new white snow. Pa always preferred going wherever was closest he couldn't see the wisdom of climbing twelve steps just to piss. When he was done he zipped up swatted the boy's hand off him went back inside. "We need some food. That church of your ma's have any?"

"People leave food off there it's for the poor."

"What's we if we ain't poor?"

"We's Baptists."

"There ain't no more Baptists in this house now she's gone. We have nothing to do with Baptists."

"Then we can't be taking food from them right?"

Pa kicked at something on the floor sent it bouncing against the wall. "Dang it I'm hungry."

"Me too."

"Then get us something go down to Holly's Market here's a dollar you buy something little and steal something big know what I mean?"

"I guess. Pa?"

"Do as you're told."

The boy grabbed his heaviest jacket off the hook by the door and went out into the cool blue morning. The world was cleaner than he ever saw it. He tramped through the snow trying to recall the particulars Pa taught him about stealing. If you got a dollar in your pocket you ordered something like coffee Holly would grind it while you strolled around whistling sticking things here and there in your jacket then put down your dollar take your coffee everything looked fine. Thing was the boy knew he couldn't stand in front of Holly not looking like a wolf caught with hen feathers stuck in his mouth. The boy favored just plain sneaking in stealing then sneaking out. In summer it was a cinch to get inside and not be seen `cause the door was open and the bells didn't jangle to call attention to yourself. In winter you had to play it smart wait till somebody left then walk in before the door shut behind them. The boy waited outside Hollingsworth's Grocery and Produce kicking clumps of snow nodding at people passing by. Then the door opened the boy could see Holly in the back stacking boxes. Mrs. Pemberton came out the boy went in. Silent as the dust he sneaked along the produce up went his hand grabbed a bunch of carrots. Onions was in a bin down low the boy didn't like them but he knew his pa did frying next to sausage so he took two. Now where did Holly keep the sausages? The boy took one step put his hand on a fat sausage the board creaked.

"Little critter!" It was Holly coming down the aisle with the broom dragging across the floor. The boy jumped out of the way like a grasshopper and scooted down the other side. "Where did you get to?" The broom kept coming the boy crept around the end of the aisle back down past the beans. "You stop now!" The boy kept running looking back he tripped into the soups stacked high they rolled across the floor. He hopped up thinking he was trapped it was a miracle the door opened Mrs. Pemberton came back in yelling at Holly "Where is that vinegar I paid you for?" The boy rushed by her as fast as the wind.

* * * * *

He ran home the whole way his pa was waiting at the door with his tongue hanging out. "What did you get?"

"I got away Pa."

"You seen?"

"Holly saw me but I don't know if he knows it was me he saw."

Pa put his hands out. "Give me."

The boy felt inside his pockets and didn't feel nothing. How could that be? He remembered stuffing his jacket full and running from the broom and then knocking over the soup cans. That had to be when it happened. "Everything fell out Pa."

"Fell out where?"

"At Holly's I fell getting away and the onions and carrots and sausage must have dropped out."

"You let sausage slip through your fingers?" Pa raised his hand the boy closed his eyes `cause he didn't want to see it as well as feel it. Pa's hand stung the boy's face. "I can't believe you come home with nothing." The boy opened his eyes didn't know what was going to happen next. "Stop looking like some dumb critter caught in the lights your ma always looked like that." The boy tried to look different Pa swung anyway the boy ducked and ran down the hall saw the basement door open slipped in there just as Pa kicked it shut behind him. The boy found a hiding place behind the old coal bin stayed there listening. After a while he heard something overhead then the front door opening. He crept up the steps turned the doorknob it didn't move. "Pa?" Nothing answered. "The door's locked." He tried the door again it didn't open again. "Pa?" He drew his legs up to his chest there was nothing to do but wait.

He fell asleep woke fell asleep and woke again hearing creaking above him "Pa!" he yelled loud as he could and the door opened there was Pa and Sheriff Wills and Preacher Daniel and Roy Dickers.

Sheriff pointed at the boy. "Thought you said he ran off somewheres?"

"How's I to know the fool boy got himself stuck in the cellar?" Pa ran his hand over the jamb of the door. "Swells up in the moisture I got myself stuck down there myself a time or two. Been meaning to shave the door."

The boy came up they all stood around the little table. Sheriff said "Sam Hollingsworth says you been at his store stealing things what do you say?"

Before he could answer his pa did. "I tell you the boy has been here with me all day sitting at the table remembering his dear departed Ma. Then he got to crying and ran off I thought he went outside guess he got himself stuck in the cellar now how could he be stealing if he was stuck down there?"

"That what you say boy?"

"I say what Pa say."

Pa nodded that it was settled. "So Holly saw some boy it don't mean it was this boy." Pa drew him close.

"I'm telling you it ain't good the boy living like this" Sheriff said "thieving for you he'll get sent up to jail and you'll be to thank."

"I take care of my own and I don't much like some puffed up Sheriff come around talking like that at me and my boy it ain't lawful."

The boy knew that was exactly true a man's home was his castle.

Sheriff pulled out a cigarette took his time lighting it. "I can get the papers to take him out of here if I find him stealing anymore if he don't go to school like every other boy if you don't provide a proper home."

"You call my boy a stealer again you better show proof and as to my house I run it like I want and I teach my boy better things than school."

Roy Dickers stepped in between Pa and Sheriff surprising everybody `cause he barely spoke a word even to his wife some say it comes from taking care of the dead. Pa said Roy was dead already and just wouldn't admit it. Roy said "It's time to stop the arguing and take care of the deceased."

He started for the stairs but Pa caught his arm. "I told you me and the boy will do right by her."

"You can't just drop her into the ground. There's a proper way."

"The Law telling people how to die now?"

"I guess you could say it is" Roy said. "The Law of this county says she got to be buried in a box clear of all streams and people and I got to certify she ain't diseased and just what she died of."

"She'd a died of boredom long before if she'd lived with you" Pa said.

"Maybe so" Roy said not getting flustered at all.

"It ain't right to step between the dead and her family" the Reverend said. That was one for the record books the Reverend siding with Pa's opinion. "It's God's Law that the body be buried by her loved ones."

"Then God's Law or Man's Law got to give" Sheriff laid it straight.

Pa walked to the front door opened it and invited everybody nice as you please to get out.

Sheriff put on his cap flicked his cigarette out the door. "I'm telling you I'll be back to take that boy if you don't clean up this house make it fit for a child."

Pa laughed at Sheriff pushed the door shut after him then turned on the boy. "You go off come back with nothing to eat and bring trouble to my house. You ain't worth the keeping I should just let them take you" he said slapping his hand at the boy's face turning it red and hot.

* * * * *

"Get up! Get up! Lazy men spending half the day under covers."

A woman's voice from downstairs stung the boy awake it was just like a spider biting your ear. You were bitten and there was no way to get free until that black crawling thing had got good and full of your blood.

"I never seen anything like it men folk bedding in the sun already risen wood to be chopped furniture to be set right might think it was a rest home for the lame."

The boy stumbled in his white nightshirt to the top of the stairs met Pa dragging the quilt behind him side by side they looked down there was Cousin Sarah looking up. "Well aren't you two a sight" she said "like something that's been stuck under the porch for a couple of years. Don't you got a kind word for Sarah?"

Pa was lucky to grunt at you before a swig of whiskey. The boy knew how to be polite he said "Morning Cousin Sarah."

"Get a move on" she said "the day's a wasting." Pa cleared his throat like it was his stomach coming up and spit on the floor at his feet. Cousin Sarah surprised them both just laughed like that was a fine joke. "Hurry now I bought the fixings for a good hot breakfast."

Pa turned back to the room at the end of the hall which he'd been sleeping in since Ma took dead. He pulled the quilt with him mumbling "We's in for it now boy."

Cousin Sarah was in the habit of dropping in every couple months seeing as how she only lived down the road a few miles. She weren't really anybody's cousin except Ma's and a distant one at that. Pa said she was so distant you needed a telescope to see her. Still the day Ma took to bed she sent the boy to get Sarah they talked secret about things for a long while. Pa knew nothing about it he was shooting his rifle in the mountains at anything that moved.

Pa sure changed his tune about Sarah when he came down saw the food spread in front of them. There was bacon and eggs steaming hot coffee biscuits dripping with cheese the boy couldn't imagine anything better. After it was all gone Pa pulled the cloth from his neck wiped his lips content as he ever was. The boy felt fine himself had just enough room for squeezing one more biscuit in his mouth.

"Sarah" Pa said "I should have hitched up with you when I had the chance you are the finest..." but he didn't get all the words out `cause she opened the oven pulled out a cherry pie. Well Ma used to call him

Cherry Pa for how much he liked it that was before she told him you take one more drink of whiskey no more pie. Pa thought it over at the time clearly thinking it was unfair to put a man through such a choice. Whiskey won out but it was close that's how much Pa liked cherry pie. And here it was with no strings attached. He ate two big pieces then grabbed for Sarah as she passed by gave her a kiss on her neck.

"Such a fuss over a simple pie" she said squirming free. Pa kept up the fuss his hands gripped the back of her held her tight his mouth worked his way down the middle of her. The boy couldn't believe what he was seeing his fingers forgot they were holding a fork it banged to the floor. Pa drew himself back from Cousin Sarah as she went about clearing the table.

"I was expecting to hear the minute she passed" Sarah said "I should have been notified."

"We was gonna" Pa said. "Things the way they was takes a few days getting straight."

"Well getting straight is what Sarah's all about" she said piling up the dishes in the sink. "We're going to start with washing you up boy." He looked to his Pa to get out of it but Pa just nodded that this was the price they had to pay for cherry pie. "You go up draw the water in the tub" Sarah said "I'll be along in a minute see you do it right."

The boy went upstairs into the bathroom put in the plug turned on the water. He sat on the edge twisting the hot and cold spigots back and forth getting the temperature just right then Cousin Sarah came bursting in the door. "Off with those clothes and don't be bashful I've seen it all before." The boy pulled off the straps to his overalls pulled the shirt over his head then turned away from Cousin Sarah shucked everything and climbed in. "Whew the filth that's on you" Sarah cried out "you're more dirt than boy." He took up the soap started rubbing himself but Sarah grabbed the bar out of his hand rubbed it on a washcloth and then rubbed that down his arms. "You have to dig in" she said showing what she meant. He stiffened up and Sarah said "Relax boy it's not going to kill you to get clean." The soap bar fell out of her hand she reached in the water for it her fingers touched the boy's stomach started tickling. He squirmed and splashed Cousin Sarah didn't seem to care she was getting wet she kept tickling and the boy couldn't help it he started laughing himself. "Does a woman good hearing a child laugh" she said. "I bet you haven't laughed for a long time have you boy?"

* * * * *

Cousin Sarah stayed to make dinner it was as fine as breakfast. In the middle of Pa struggling to get a big piece of meat into his mouth Sarah pointed at the boy "Don't he look fresh?"

Pa swallowed. "Looks like a can of white paint fell on him."

"Some proper clothes would make him a real gentleman boy" Sarah said.

"We don't have proper clothes around here."

Sarah jumped up got the bag she'd left in Grandpa's chair all day. She opened it up there was some things from her brother Lyle a small man who didn't need clothes no more. The boy tried on the shirts and trousers not liking any of them but Sarah clapped each time she saw him in something new and Pa just laughed. When the boy finished trying on everything Sarah said "Now we got him washed and dressed it's time we fixed you up."

Pa nodded to Sarah as he'd been doing all day not really listening.

"I'll clear away the dishes you get the water going in the tub."

Pa looked up at her like he just agreed to being plugged with buckshot. "I don't need no washing."

"The boy said the same thing now look at him."

"Now it's your turn" the boy said.

Pa started for the door but Sarah played her trump card said she might heat up some more cherry pie for dessert later for a proper looking man. So Pa went upstairs Sarah followed. The boy shuffled around downstairs looking at all the mess of things Sarah had pushed to one corner. He wanted more pie. He knew he couldn't just take it but there wasn't any sin to smelling it again. He pulled back the cloth smelled deep it was like standing in a cherry orchard. After a while he went upstairs quiet as could be in his stocking feet looked in the door of the end room. There Pa was just a wet towel wrapped around him hugging Sarah. The boy meant only to think her name but it jumped out of his mouth Pa turned around saw the boy. "Well look there" Pa said "your eyes are wider than a horse's behind." He stuck one foot out to kick the door shut but Sarah stopped it. She wiggled out from Pa's hands said "That's enough of that you'll give the boy the wrong idea." She came out of the room carrying Pa's dirty clothes walked the boy down the hall and they both stopped at Ma's door looked in. "Death's a troublesome thing" she said after a while. "It's just a matter of looking at it enough times till you get used to it."

The boy nodded but he didn't believe he'd ever get used to it even if he got to watch the whole world die all around him.

* * * * *

Come morning sun shined through the window sparkling dust on the boy's face. Sitting on his bedside looking out the sound of melting snow from the roof was like ticks of the clock. He got himself dressed walked down to the bathroom to wash himself and peeked in Pa's room Pa wasn't there. He went downstairs there was Cousin Sarah scrubbing up the kitchen like she'd moved in for good. She turned around hearing the boy smiled at him said "You hungry?"

"Can't remember a time I wasn't."

"We'll fix that" she said pulling a chair out for him to sit in. "A boy growing like you needs the fuel to do it."

"Where's Pa?"

"Went out first thing" Sarah said "where does he go first thing?"

To Jake's the boy thought but Pa wouldn't want him saying he drank whiskey for breakfast. "He doesn't let me go with him so I never really seen where he goes" which wasn't lying.

Cousin Sarah moved the steam kettle off the burner. "You saw us last night in his room did you?"

The boy nodded. "I didn't see much."

"You aren't old enough to understand there's a purpose behind things sometimes. I know it don't look right but I'm doing this for you and your ma."

Seemed like she was doing it for Pa but the boy didn't say that he sat there eating everything Cousin Sarah put in front of him. She poured herself more coffee then sat across from him watching. "Your pa and me known each other forever. We grew up together along with your ma you know that?" The boy shook his head. "Well it's true so I know your pa. You want something from him you got to get on his good side." The boy remembered Ma saying Pa didn't have a good side anymore but maybe he did now that she was gone. "That's what I'm doing" she said. The boy didn't understand and truly he didn't care `cause those biscuits with cheese spread on top of them were squeezing into every part of himself. Sarah reached out the boy thought she was going to wipe cheese off his lips she held his chin up. "You got your ma inside you" she said. "You grow into a fine young man given half a chance."

* * * * *

The boy did chores all day whatever Sarah asked. As night came on she said she hadn't been figuring on staying over again but guessed she could sleep in the rocker one more night she couldn't leave him alone. She found some books in the piano bench where his ma stored them books about wars and pirates and other things boys liked to hear. She took him upstairs to bed and read parts of the books to him as he laid back feeling warm listening to her till he heard the door pushed in below. Then there was a thud that would be Pa hitting the floor. He never was much for getting far into the house when he was full of whiskey.

"I'll fix that" Sarah said she got a bucket from the bathroom filled it halfway with cold water went down-stairs gave Pa fair warning he didn't get up. She threw the water on him like to drown him. The boy saw the whole thing from the top of the steps.

Pa jumped up "Woman you crazy?" he said blotting his face with his sleeve.

"A man comes falling in the house like a good for nothing he gets what's coming."

"I fall where I want to in my own house" Pa said " and I expect to wake up next morning in the same place."

"I don't abide drunkenness."

"This ain't your house to abide or not abide. How come you still here?"

"I was watching after the boy" Sarah said "in case you forgot you had one."

Pa wrung out the belly of his shirt. "You sound just like that old dead woman upstairs."

"You drove her to the grave sure as I'm standing here a Christian woman."

"A Christian whore. You come busting in this house with pie and biscuits before that woman's body is even buried remembering how we was together a long time ago. Think I'm a fool don't see what you're after?"

"You *are* a fool but mind your tongue in front of the boy."

"Mind my fist" Pa said he rushed her caught the side of her head so hard she tumbled to the floor. Then he dropped down on her like to have his way but she rolled him off Pa was too drunk to get what he wanted whatever that was.

* * * * *

Cousin Sarah took off in the dark the boy saw her walking down the road in the moonlight she whispered don't worry I'll be back. He spent the rest of the evening out of Pa's way upstairs. He could hear thumps and curses and more thumps downstairs Pa seemed to be messing up the place again. Sarah wouldn't be pleased. The boy went to his ma's room opened the door the smell kicked him in the face. He ran to the window opened it up and stuck his head out. No matter how much he liked having Ma in the house it was clear to his nose and other parts of himself that it was time she got moved on. He figured Pa would be no help he had to do it himself. He wrapped her up in the blankets pulled her off the bed she was awful stiff he dragged her to the stairs by her arms and bounced her down to the bottom and there she lay. "Pa?" he called but got no answer. He leaned his ma half against the door started looking in the mess there was Pa rising out of it. He saw Ma like you see something standing in the shadows at nightfall you don't know if you saw it or not and hoped you didn't. "What in tarnation?"

The boy couldn't see what all the surprise was about. "It's Ma she's dead don't you remember?"

Pa wiped his hand across his mouth which was dried out needing something to wetten it up. "What's she doing there?"

"I was getting her ready to go in the ground."

"Then you just keep on going with her out the door."

"She's too heavy Pa and the melting just started yesterday we need time for the ground to soften up."

Pa gave in seeing the sense of things for once. "You can keep her in here till morning then she goes in the ground" he said heading out the door himself.

The boy ran upstairs grabbed his ma's black and red afghan and her slippers and her shawl ran downstairs propped her up on the floor making her as comfortable as could be for the long dark night.

* * * *

Next morning he was sitting at the kitchen table across from his pa eating the biscuits and milk and hot cereal that Sarah left. The meal was going down fine no need to talk about anything just eat. A knock at the door made him straighten up `cause it sounded like the knock of trouble. Pa took his time pulling up his suspenders shuffling over to the door opened it there was Sheriff Wills again with Cousin Sarah behind him and Roy Dickers behind her. "We'd like to come in have a talk" Sheriff said.

Pa smiled all polite. "It's a pleasure to have a visit from the Sheriff and my good Cousin Sarah." He nodded at Roy coming in too.

They came into the kitchen found seats around the table Pa even offered coffee. "Now" Sheriff said "Sarah's made some charges."

"Charges?" Pa said.

"Said you laid hands on her last night."

"Well if that's all I confess to that."

"You confess to hitting her?"

"Wheweee that's a strange thing to say. You say that Sarah?"

Sarah gripped her bag she carried everywhere tight on her lap like she was afraid Pa would snatch it from her. "I do."

"Well now why would I want to go and hit my dear wife's old Cousin Sarah?"

Sheriff resettled himself in his seat clearly not wanting to come out with it. "So's you could use her for a woman you were going to force her."

Pa hooted at that. "Well don't the tale get stranger every time you hear it. I ain't never had to force a woman to get it."

"Then how do you go explaining this bruise" Sheriff pointed on Sarah's face.

"Must have been the unfamiliar kitchen. Bumping her head here and there on the cabinet I can see how it happened." Sarah shook her head like don't that beat all but Pa kept on. "Now I don't deny we was upstairs together last night. And God judge me" Pa said holding his hand up like he was taking an oath "we were mourning together holding each other. The boy chanced to see it. Look like I was forcing her then boy?" The boy didn't answer up immediately. "Was she yelling and screaming like I was forcing her?"

"She weren't" the boy said.

"I wouldn't trust that boy not to lie straight into the face of Jesus" Sheriff said. "As for you doing such things in the same house your wife barely gone cold."

"You got no right to talk `bout my boy or me like that we been patient letting you in. I've a mind to take you to court for these accusings and name callings." Pa turned on Sarah then. "I'd take you to court too tell the whole county what a church-going woman named Sarah Wilby does when the shades are pulled down right after her cousin died."

"I never heard such" Sarah said.

"Wouldn't surprise me she got to you too" Pa said to Sheriff.

Sheriff didn't like that he jabbed his finger into the air at Pa. "I've been to Judge Grady he knows this isn't a fit place for a boy."

Pa laughed loud. "Ain't no way on this God-wretched earth you can take a boy from his rightful pa no matter what this woman says I did. Ain't the Law wonderful?"

Sheriff said "Right now the Law's going to make sure the body of the deceased is taken care of proper." He moved toward the stairs but Pa thumbed into the corner there was Mama sitting like some giant stuffed animal. Sarah gasped Roy looked like now he'd seen it all. "Take her out" Sheriff said. Roy took the bag he was carrying unzipped it got Mama in zipped it up and carried her over his shoulder. Everybody said Roy Dickers was stronger than he looked. The boy didn't know where they were taking her he couldn't see no reason they didn't just put her in the garden which she liked more than any place. Sheriff said "It's the letter of the Law to do it this way." Well then the boy said to himself the Law's got some mighty crooked letters in it if a body can't be buried where it wants to.

* * * * *

By evening Sarah's food had run out the boy took to hunting around the kitchen again. On the floor next to the trash bin there was a piece of bread he bent over reached for it. Something else moved toward it too a shining black rat. The creature got the bread dragged it over the boy's bare toes sent a chill up his spine he'd never forget.

"Pa!" the boy shouted "Git your gun."

Pa came in the kitchen kind of slow. "What's all the crying about?"

"A rat the size of a cat Pa like to drag me off instead of the bread."

"Then he would have deserved you."

"Scared me out of my pants."

"There's been rats in this house long as I can remember why you scared now?"

"I never had one wrestle my dinner from me."

"Well you got to think of it as their place too they got to eat."

Pa had a strange way of seeing things sometimes and being hospitable to rats was one of them. "How'd you like your meal thieved by one?"

"Got to make them scared of you boy. Strongest one gets the food. You understand that?"

"Understanding don't fill me up none."

"You sassin' me?" The boy shrugged that maybe he was maybe he wasn't. Pa pulled his favorite black and white checked coat off the hook. "I'm going down to Jake's get something to warm up my insides."

The boy jumped to his feet. "Take me too Pa."

"Can't be taking a boy to a drinking house."

"I'll wait outside you can stay long as you want."

"You'd freeze your ears off."

"I'd be fine Pa don't leave me with the rats."

"That's just why I am leaving you it ain't no good a boy growing up scared of rats driving him from his own house. You got to learn to live with them."

"I will Pa just not tonight."

He didn't bother answering buttoned up his coat walked out the front door.

Ain't nothing silenter than a house just left. Makes you feel like there ain't nobody coming back ever. The front room was getting dark the boy knew rats like the dark `cause they can see just as if it was daytime boys don't like the dark. He found some matches lit the oil lamp and sat up on the stool his legs pulled up to the top rung. Maybe rats ain't so bad they never hurt Pa. That one just snitched some bread ain't nothing to scare you losing a bit of food. But when the bread ran out for the rats what would they try to eat next? It was darkening awful fast. The oil lamp wasn't doing more than casting big shadows where things could hide. The boy pulled the chain to the floor lamp tall as him. The light didn't switch on. He traced the cord it was plugged in so he screwed the bulb tight still nothing. Something rubbed his ankle he jumped into the air and he would have stayed up forever if he could have. The boy landed on the floor hurried to his room skinned off his clothes pulled his nightshirt on over his head. He tried the lamp next to his bed and just as he feared it didn't turn on something strange was happening maybe the rats found a way to stop light. His teeth got to chattering his knees shaking like a caught rabbit. And there weren't a thing to be done except wait and listen and be scared some more. He pulled his pillow round about his ears and held tight so he wouldn't have to hear anything that scared him. He wished even though nothing ever happened that he wished for he wished that there was some way a boy could wish himself somewhere else. He closed his eyes and hummed himself a tune he just made up and held the pillow fast to his ears. Then there was something trying to pull the pillow off him had to be the rats he kept his eyes closed so as not to see them. The something kept pulling and pulling he couldn't hold the pillow any longer it came flying off him.

"What's got into you boy?"

It was Pa it was Pa. "Pa!"

"Who else you expecting?"

The boy grabbed his neck and just about pulled his pa in bed with him. "You came back Pa I knew you wouldn't leave me with the rats."

Pa freed himself and sat on the bed. "You still got that dollar I gave you for Holly's or did that fall out of your trousers too?"

"I got it" the boy said jumping out of the covers digging into his trouser pockets handed over the dollar.

Pa stood up put the bill in his own pocket as the boy crawled back in bed. Suddenly he feared that with the dollar Pa would go now to Jake's. "You aren't leaving again are you? Please don't go."

Pa licked his lips said "Dang it all right I'll stay can't buy more than a beer with a dollar anyway Jake's getting stingy with his credit."

The boy lay back on his bed let his eyes close now he could sleep. It sure was good having Pa home. The rats knew not to mess with him.

* * * * *

The boy woke up feeling empty again like an egg blown out for dyeing. Still he weren't crying hungry which is how Ma said she felt at times when she was growing up. Remembering her made him remember something else. He went downstairs looked behind the piano the boy stuck his arm in couldn't reach what he wanted. He pushed on the piano all his might the thing moved a few inches. He stretched himself thin as he could wedging his face in between the wall and the piano finally got his hand on it. He pulled out the picture he'd done of his ma full of dust it was. He blew it clean and there was her face staring out at him plain as day. She said she couldn't pay ten dollars for a better likeness of herself. He remembered her saying that.

Pa looked up from the rocker where he was rocking slowly. The boy said "Pa where's Ma's soul?"

"What're you reminding me of that woman first thing the morning? I tell you she didn't have a soul and that's the truth so you don't have to worry about where it went." Pa pointed at what the boy was holding. "What's that fool thing?"

"A picture. I drew it."

"Let me see" Pa said with his hand out.

The boy put the drawing behind his back. "You won't like it Pa you don't want to see it."

"All right." Pa stood up casual as could be then grabbed around the boy snatched the picture.

"Pa!" the boy yelled and fell to his knees "give it back."

"I'll give it back" he said ripping the picture first one way then the other. He let the pieces fall into the boy's hands. "I want nothing remaining in this house reminds me of that woman and the miserable eleven years living with her. I told you that."

"This is the only thing I have left of her" the boy cried "the one thing."

"Now you have four things so's I did you a favor."

The boy didn't see it that way he fitted the pieces on the table then took some tape and put his ma back together again. It didn't look so good with the jagged cuts running this way and that across her face but you could tell it was her if you already knew it was.

"Pa?"

"What's it now?"

"Why don't you ever like ma?"

He looked angry at the boy then grabbed him by the shoulders. "You only knew her as your ma she was supposed to be a wife to me she weren't ever a wife to me after she had you."

He didn't know what Pa meant by that. He wanted to ask but Pa was staring deep into the boy's face not saying anything the boy got scared and shook himself free.

* * * * *

When Pa left he said you chop some wood get a fire going by the time I get back whenever that is. So the boy found some old logs under the porch pulled them out set them on the chopping block and split them clean through the way Pa taught him. He liked chopping wood.

"Easy swing you have there son." The words came up behind him it was Preacher Daniel surprising the boy he almost lost his grip and let the axe fly. Pa wouldn't like anybody else calling him son he knew that he said hello trying to be polite as Ma taught him.

"Your pa isn't inside?"

"No sir."

"And he wouldn't be coming back soon?"

"Hard to say."

"Well let's you and me get to talking where it's warm." The boy gathered up an armful of logs and the Preacher did the same they went in side by side stacked the wood next to the fireplace. "Now boy" the Preacher said then shook his head like something just came to him "I been wondering since I came to this town everybody calls you boy don't you have a Christian name it don't seem right calling you that?"

The boy didn't say `cause his ma made him swear he wouldn't tell anyone he had a name only Cousin Sarah knew.

"How'd it come you don't have a name ain't a boy in the world without a name?"

"Ma wanted to give me a church name."

"That's baptism."

"Pa said no boy of his was gonna get a church

name."

Preacher said "We'll have to think on that won't we?" It was one of those questions the Preacher always asked that weren't meant to be answered. "Maybe since you're almost grown now your pa would let you pick your own." The boy laughed at the idea of picking your name like picking a dog's name he knew right off what he'd call himself Rebel Two. "But that isn't why I came visiting. I wanted to talk about your mother. When a body dies like her a fine Christian woman you know where her soul goes?"

"She had no soul."

The Preacher's eyes opened up like they'd seen something big and growling in the night. "Who told you that?"

"Pa."

The Preacher considered for a minute. "You're old enough to know a Pa can be wrong sometimes your mother had a soul and it went to heaven. But there's another part of her that didn't go anywhere."

The boy thought hard but didn't know what the Preacher was talking about. "Which part is that?"

"It's the part where you remember her. I'm telling you her passing doesn't have to be a leaving you can still feel like your mother's right beside you. And you should be trying to do what she'd think is right because she's watching all the time just as I'm watching you this moment." The boy knew what the Preacher meant it was like God watching you even though you couldn't watch God. "Some things you been doing Sheriff spoke to me about your ma wouldn't like the looks of them would she?"

"No sir."

"You going to try to do better?"

The boy nodded and the Preacher took his hands. "Let us pray. Lord this boy needs Your help on his way to becoming a fine young man a credit to his community and the Kingdom of God. Now his mother's gone to join You for everlasting life in heaven. His father Lord save him is a man not living in the light of Jesus..."

"Lord save the Preacher!" Pa bust in the front door like a man stepped on a bee hole. He picked up Grandpa's big chair raised it over his head.

"There's no call for violence" Preacher said letting go the boy's hands standing up backing away. Pa roared the boy closed his eyes the Preacher covered his head. The boy heard a crash he opened his eyes expecting to see the Preacher bleeding red like a dead squirrel. But there was Pa lying flat on his back dragged to the floor by the weight of the chair. Ma said drinking gets a man in a rage sometimes he's got the strength of Samson. But one drink more he's like Samson his hair cut off having no more strength than a newborn. Pa couldn't even lift himself up.

The Preacher stepped over the squirming body

stopped at the door and said to the boy "Remember your mother's watching."

"Git me up!" Pa yelled from the floor where he spent much of his life. The boy lifted off the chair and pulled him up. He said "I don't go to church I don't expect the church coming to me." The Preacher didn't hear he was leaving through the door whistling. Pa hated people whistling as much as anything.

* * * * *

Knocking came loud from downstairs the boy hurried down opened up the front door. Well if it wasn't Cousin Sarah carrying a basket in both arms with a linen over the top smelling like fresh baked bread. He hadn't expected to see her again in this house not since Pa bruised her. "Don't just stand there help a lady" she said breezing into the house.

He took the basket from her arms set it on the table then took her coat off and hung it up all the time eyeing the basket. "What's you got in there Cousin Sarah?"

"Just something to fill a boy's stomach is all" she pulled back the cloth giving him a peek. He liked to faint at the sight of fresh baked oat bread, orange jam, applesauce and a large bottle of milk. She pulled the linen back over. "First things first. Where would the man of the house be I'd like a word with him."

"You mean Pa?"

"I do." The boy pointed into the back corner of the

kitchen where the man of the house was slumped over on himself. About all you could see of his face was his nose which Ma used to call it a right distinctive piece of God's work. "Well ain't that a fine example" Sarah said walking up to him lifting his head by his hair. His eyes opened a little but they might as well of stayed shut seeing nothing. "A lady comes all dressed up for a visit finds the man looking like this." She turned back saw the boy poking in the basket.

"I'm sorry Cousin Sarah I'm so hungry I couldn't keep my hand down any longer."

"Go ahead then. If that sorry excuse for a man misses out it's his own doing. You eat your fill."

The boy dove in with both hands but Sarah pulled him away set him down at his place at the table got him a knife fork and spoon told him to eat proper. Then she took the rag hanging over the spigot ran some cold water on it and squeezed it out on Pa's head. He woke up soon enough saw Sarah rubbing his eyes he couldn't believe it. "You come back for more you fool woman?"

She said "You don't scare Sarah I get what I want in the end."

"I'll give you what you want in the end" Pa said swiping the air in front of him she stepped out of his reach.

"Start that again you won't hear nothing of the 857 dollars."

That got Pa's attention. "What 857 dollars?"

"Get yourself over to the table I'll tell you about it." Pa pulled himself up by the counter steadied himself and wobbled over to the chair and sank down. "Some oat bread?" Sarah asked polite as can be taking the loaf out of the basket handing it over to him.

Pa pulled off a hunk and heaped on some orange jam. "Now about the 857..."

"Applesauce?" Sarah said pulling out a tall glass jar of it. "I put it up last fall."

Pa nodded and spooned some out. "...this 857 dollars you was mentioning."

"That's what I'm coming to. Think you could find some use for 857 dollars?"

That was like asking Pa if he could use another whiskey. "Any man can't figure out how to use money like that don't have much of a head on him."

"Well" Sarah said "don't you think it's curious that I'm talking about 857 dollars exactly and not 850 or 900 dollars?"

Pa scratched his chin. "I guess it is kind of peculiar."

Sarah unfolded a piece of paper she had in her hand. "Sheriff told me that's how much you owe at Hollingsworth's and Jake's and some other places around town. You also got taxes to settle on this place and you might want to pay your electricity bill if you're figuring on having lights again."

"What's all that to you?"

"I got 857 dollars saved up could get you out of owing."

Pa looked at her straight. "I ain't beholden to no man."

"Well" said Sarah holding up her list of Pa's debts like evidence "I'd say you are beholden to quite a few men. The question is would you rather be beholden to one woman your kin?"

"What kind of beholden would this be?"

Sarah nodded that the conversation had finally come around to the important part. "I ain't never had the opportunity of a husband you know."

Pa jumped out of his seat slapped his thigh twirled around twice and sat down again more movement than the boy'd seen in him for years. "I just got rid of one wife you think I'm crazy enough to try on another?"

Now it was Sarah's turn she held her sides and laughed like the boy never saw a woman. "Lord Almighty you think `cause I let you hug me one night I'd make a habit of it?"

"You liked it" Pa said "don't say you didn't."

Sarah shrugged not saying she did or didn't. "I let you hold me for old times and `cause I wanted something from you that's all."

"What do you want?" Pa said looking kind of angry now.

"Like I was saying I haven't had the opportunity for a husband which is the normal way of getting children if you get my meaning." Sarah tipped her head toward the boy.

"Well don't that beat all" Pa said hitting the table with his fist. "I thought you was fixing to buy me here I'm beat out by my own boy."

"It ain't buying him" Sarah said. "It's making an arrangement that's good for everybody. This boy shouldn't be living in a house like this no food on the table the mother dead the father drunk."

Pa started talking about how strong the boy was and how he was the spitting image of himself as a young man when he cleaned up and how he didn't cost much to feed. The boy straightened up in his chair trying to look 857 dollars worth. "This one's my only child" Pa said patting him on the head. "I don't got no other. You asking me to give up my own blood. It's like cutting off my arm and handing it to you. There ain't a price high enough to buy a man's arm or his boy" Pa said. He stuffed more bread in his mouth. "Least not 857 dollars."

Sarah stared him down so hard he had to look away. "I'll pay off your debts that's 857 dollars and I'll give you another 43 you can do with it what you want probably drink through it in a week makes it 900 even."

"That's better" Pa said "but it takes some thinking

about what you're asking." He scratched his chin a while. "Make it 1,000 and I won't have to think at all."

Sarah shook her head she said "I can't believe a man would bargain over his child. His ma begged me to do anything to save the boy I'll bring you 1,000 dollars cash tomorrow."

"`Course if…" Pa started but Sarah held up her hand for him to stop.

"Ask for one cent more I'll take my offer home with me and get the Law to take the boy away from you then you get nothing." Pa saw the sense of closing the deal fast he put out his hand over the table Sarah shook it and just like that the boy belonged to somebody else.

"Come on then Adam" she said and at first he didn't know who she was talking to he had never heard his name spoken out loud like that. She tapped him on the shoulder and he jumped up put on the coat she was holding out to him this meant he was leaving. At the door the boy turned to wave goodbye but Pa's head was slumping on the kitchen table his eyes already gone closed as if forever.